The Fighting Four

OTHER SAGEBRUSH LARGE PRINT WESTERNS BY
MAX BRAND®

The Abandoned Outlaw: A Western Trio
The City in the Sky
Crossroads
The Desert Pilot
Dust Across the Range
Farewell Thunder Moon
Fire Brain
Fugitives' Fire
The Legend of Thunder Moon
Luck
The Night Horseman
The Oath of Office
The One-Way Trail: A Western Trio
The Pride of Tyson
The Quest of Lee Garrison
Safety McTee: A Western Trio
Slumber Mountain: A Western Trio
Soft Metal: A Western Trio
Tales of the Wild West: A Western Trio
Thunder Moon and Red Wind
Thunder Moon and the Sky People
Two Sixes: A Western Trio
The Ghost Rides Tonight!
The Untamed
The Valley of Jewels

The Fighting Four

MAX BRAND®

Sagebrush
Large Print Westerns

Library of Congress Cataloging-in-Publication Data

Brand, Max, 1892-1944.
   The fighting four / Max Brand
      p.   cm.
   ISBN 1-57490-476-0 (lg. print : hardcover)
      p.   cm.
   1. Sheriffs—Fiction. 2. Large type books. I. Title: Fighting
4. II. Title.

PS3511.A87F475 2003
813'.52—dc21   2003004341

Cataloging in Publication Data is available from
the British Library and the National Library of Australia.

Sagebrush Large Print Westerns are published in the United
States and Canada by Thomas T. Beeler, Publisher, PO Box 659,
Hampton Falls, New Hampshire 03844-0659. ISBN 1-57490-476-0

Published in the United Kingdom, Eire, and the Republic of
South Africa by Isis Publishing Ltd, 7 Centremead, Osney
Mead, Oxford OX2 0ES England. ISBN 0-7531-6911-8

Published in Australia and New Zealand by Bolinda Publishing
Pty Ltd, 17 Mohr Street, Tullamarine, Victoria, Australia, 3043
ISBN 1-74030-918-9

Manufactured by Sheridan Books in Chelsea, Michigan.

The Fighting Four

THE ELKDALE BANK

THE FIRST NATIONAL BANK OF ELKDALE WAS ROBBED at two thirty in the afternoon of an early spring day. It was still so early in the season that it was possible to see a flush of green on the lower slopes of the hills, and the head of Iron Mountain, in the farther distance, was snow-hooded far down to the breadth of the shoulders.

It was a still, hushed afternoon, with thin clouds chasing one another cheerfully across the sky, and the air above the earth perfectly motionless except when a little whirlpool started in the increasing heat and sucked up a whirling pyramid of dust.

At two o'clock that afternoon Oliver Wayland, the cashier of the First National, took advantage of a moment when there was no customer in the building and went into the office of the president, William Rucker, carrying a big, flat parcel under his arm.

Rucker was a burly, fierce old man, and he looked up with a scowl at the interruption; but when he saw the fragile form of his cashier, the lean, handsome face, and the big, pale structure of the brow, he turned his scowl into a smile. He liked his cashier. He liked him so well that he was pleased by the approaching marriage between Wayland and his daughter, May Rucker.

Wayland pulled the wrapping paper of the parcel away and revealed a big, framed photograph, saying: "This came in the mail today, Mr. Rucker. I suppose we'll put it on the wall, and I wanted to ask you where."

He held up before the eyes of Rucker the photograph, which showed a tall man with big shoulders and a patiently smiling face standing at the side of a great stallion which had his head thrown high and looked a challenge from the picture.

Under the photograph was written, in a bold, strong hand, these words: "From the town of Crow's Nest to every lover of justice and law in the West. We hope the face of Jim Silver, who saved us, will become just as well known as his life."

Rucker looked at the photograph silently for a moment. He was a rough fellow, was Rucker. He had not been a banker all his days. He had begun his days by working on a ranch, and he still knew the working end of a hunting knife or a Colt revolver. He stuck out his big, square jaw and scowled again.

"A picture of Jim Silver, eh?" said he. "What the devil is he doing? Running himself for office? Dog catcher, or something?"

"Not dog catcher," said the cashier. "Wolf catcher would be more like it."

"It would, would it?" asked Rucker. "I suppose that you're in favor of cluttering up the wall space of the bank with pictures like this?"

"A picture of Jim Silver," said the cashier, "would look good to me, no matter where it might be hung."

"Well," said Rucker, "what the devil good does a picture like that do?"

It was, at this time, about twenty minutes before the robbery of the bank took place, and there was a touch of prophecy in the voice of Wayland as he answered.

"Well, I think that crooks would go mare slowly if they saw a picture of Jim Silver. And every honest, man would feel that he had one friend in the world. After all; honesty is what a bank wants to encourage."

"Jim Silver," remarked the bank president, "has done more for law and order than any other man in the West,

2

I suppose. There's only one thing you can be sure of—that he'd hate to see pictures of himself being spread around the countryside. But you can't blame that town of Crow's Nest for wanting to make a fuss about him. Go hang that picture up where everybody can see it, will you?"

"I'll hang it up where I can have a good look at it myself every minute of the day," said Wayland.

"Why?" asked Rucker curiously. "Why d'you want to look at it yourself, Oliver?"

"Because," answered Wayland slowly, as though he were thinking out the thing for himself bit by bit, "because thinking about a fellow like Jim Silver helps any man to do his duty. Helps any man to be ready to die on the job."

"What's the matter?" asked Rucker. "Are you afraid of robbers?"

"There's more hard cash in our safe than we have a right to keep there," answered Wayland.

"Are you afraid of it?" exclaimed Rucker. "I'm the one to say how much is safe with us. Now trot along and get to your work. Don't dictate bank policies to me, young man!"

The temper of Rucker was always uncertain. As it exploded this time, with a roar, Wayland retreated from the office to the outer corridor that ran past the windows of the bank.

Rucker would get over his temper before long. But the fact was that the safe was old and worthless, and inside of it there was over a half million in cash. Wayland had reason to worry about it; Rucker had even better reason.

Wayland got a chair, pulled it close to the wall facing his cashier's window, and then, climbing onto the chair,

3

he tacked up the photograph of Jim Silver and Silver's horse, Parade. Hal Parson, the ruddy old janitor, who stood by to assist, delayed matters by dropping his handful of nails when they were wanted. As Wayland got down from the chair, he smelled the pungency of Parson's breath, and said to him in a low tone:

"Hal, you're tight again.''

"Tight?" answered Hal Parson. "Who says that I'm tight? I'll break the jaw of the gent that calls me tight."

"*I* say you're tight," answered the cashier. "You're full of whisky. It's the second time this month that you've had your skin full. And I warned you the other day that the very next break would be the last one."

The janitor lowered his big head like a bull about to charge. He made no answer, because he knew that the young, pale-faced cashier was his best friend in the world.

"I ought to march you into the office of Mr. Rucker right now," went on Wayland. "I ought to let him see your condition, because a fellow like you is not safe around a bank. Remember what I'm telling you. I'm responsible for the way the things go on in this bank—outside of the president's office. And I can't let this happen to you again. Now go out and run some cold water over your head. Then come back, and I'll take a look at you."

The janitor went off, his head down, growling to himself. And the cashier turned his head and saw a girl in a straw hat and a straw-colored dress smiling toward him as she stood with her hand on the knob of the door of the president's office.

That was May Rucker. He went to her happily. She was a rather plain girl. When she grew older, she would look a bit too much like her big-jawed father. But at the

4

moment she had the beauty of youth and much smiling, and she had a good, steady pair of eyes that would never grow old or dim.

"What's the matter, Oliver?" she asked him. "Is there something wrong with poor old Hal Parson again?"

"You know what's generally wrong with him," said the cashier. "I like him as much as you do, but he's got to reform!"

"*I'll* take him in hand," said the girl. "He's done a lot for me. If I talk to him, maybe he'll do something for himself."

She gave Wayland her smile again and went on into her father's office, while the cashier turned back down the corridor and went toward his own cage, which contained the great, old-fashioned safe. He never looked at that safe without wondering how the yeggs who had traveled the West in search of easy marks had not picked out this as a choice opportunity.

He was thinking, as he walked, that life was simple for him—a straight path to a goal that could not fail to be reached, unless he died suddenly. He could not help marrying May Rucker. She could not help inheriting her father's interest in the bank. And so the whole business would one day rest entirely in his hands.

He felt that he would be competent to handle the affairs of the community. He did, not look upon banking as a means of bleeding patrons who were in debt to the institution. He looked upon banking as a means of pumping lifeblood through a developing region. And he felt that he knew the men and the industries which were worth support in that part of the world. He had been a cowpuncher, lumberjack, and various other things, it was chiefly his lack of physical strength that had forced him to take up clerical work. Half of his nature was still

5

out roaming the highlands or riding the desert ranges.

So he turned into his big cage, fenced around with the bronze-gilt bars of steel. And again his glance fell on the old safe. He shook his head, as he nearly always did when he looked toward the old, inefficient structure.

He looked out of the rear window over the roofs of the town toward the big sea of the mountains, made dark by the rugged growth of the pines.

They seemed to him to be in motion, sweeping toward the town of Elkdale. A strange sense of gloom came slowly over the heart of the cashier as he got back on his stool before his barred window.

This was only a little over five minutes before the bank was robbed.

THE ROBBERY

AT THIS SAME TIME, FOUR RIDERS CAME JOGGING quietly down the main street of Elkdale and dismounted in front of the watering troughs that were lined up before the general-merchandise store of P. V. Wilkie. The horses at once stretched their heads toward the water, but one of the four, the smallest man of the lot, with a pinched, rat-like face, gathered the reins and jerked on them to keep the heads of the horses in the air.

Those horses wanted water, and since the riders had just come into town, there was no good reason why they would have to be kept from it, unless the riders expected to be leaving the town again at high speed before many minutes had passed. However, none of the idlers in the street paid any attention, neither did they notice the way in which Jimmy Lovell presently pretended to tether the horses to the hitch rack and made no progress in his work.

In the meantime, the other three went down to the corner, turned across the street, and walked back up the other side of it to the big double doors that opened into the First National Bank of Elkdale, where half a million dollars in cash rested in the safe.

Joe Mantry was young, light-stepping, handsome. He was as reckless as a bull-terrier puppy, and he had the light of a fighting terrier in his brown eyes. Dave Lister was tall, and had a long, pale face. The leader, Phil Bray, was a handsome fellow in a way, but there seemed to be something missing from the center of his face; one could hardly say what.

It was Bray who walked ahead of the others to the cashier's window and laid the barrel of a big Colt .45 on the sill of the window.

"Shove up your hands and keep your mouth shut," said Bray.

In the banking room there was only one other man, the teller. He was a grizzled man with only one leg. The lack of a leg was what kept him inside a bank instead of out in the mountains.

Dave Lister covered the teller.

Poor Oliver Wayland looked up at the savage eyes of the robber who was before him, and above the head of Phil Bray to the picture which his own hands had lately nailed against the wall at a convenient level. He saw there the smiling, good-looking face of Jim Silver, looking far too young for the fame which he had won. Wayland had nailed up the picture, thinking that this would be an example to him and to the others in the bank. Silver was the sort of a man who preferred death to a failure in any line of duty.

Now what would he, Oliver Wayland, do?

7

He though of duty and honor—but when he thought of moldering death, he thought also of young May Rucker.

"You fool, get your mitts up," said Phil Bray.

Slowly the cashier raised his hands.

May Rucker and the sweetness of life—that was what he thought of.

From the tail of his eye he saw the old teller standing, reaching his hands toward the ceiling. In the farther distance the third of the bandits was circling through the end gate and hurrying toward the safe.

Was it possible that the bank was to be robbed without the lifting of a single voice to give the alarm?

There was no doubt in the mind of Wayland now. He understood that the faint smile on the lips of Jim Silver was caused by his contempt for the weakness of ordinary mortals. But Jim Silver was a hero, and Oliver Wayland was not. Heroes find something to do because their brains are not frozen up with terror; but in the mind of Wayland there was nothing but the spinning shadow of terror and of shame. He could think of nothing at all.

Behind him he heard the hands of the third of the robbers busy at the safe.

Half a million in hard cash—and the minutes were running on faster than the cold sweat ran on the face of Wayland! He heard the subdued clinking of steel against steel as drawer after drawer of the safe was pulled out.

What difference did it make—a good safe or an old and crazy one, so long as the hired men of the bank did not have the courage necessary for their jobs?

Every minute was long enough to drive Wayland to madness. And then something stirred at the rear of the bank. A door opened—the rear door. And old Hal

8

Parson walked in, his head dark, his hair shining from the recent ducking which he had given himself to regain his sobriety.

"Stick up your hands, brother!" called Dave Lister, the tall, pale bandit. "Stick 'em up—and pronto!"

Hal Parson had seen what was happening with slow and dazed eyes. He started to lift his hands. Then he was aware of that picture on the wall that seemed to say to Hal Parson that courage is always worth while, and chances are worth taking, so long as they are in a good cause.

He saw his friend and patron, Wayland, the cashier, with his long, slender arms stretched above his head, and he remembered in a flash the thousand benefactions that he had received from that man. He remembered the kindness, the money loans, the warnings, the good advice he had often received from Oliver Wayland. And he realized that the result of this day might well be the ruin of the bank and therefore the loss of Wayland's position.

At the same time, Hal Parson recalled the stub-nosed revolver which he carried on his hip. He got that revolver out with one jerking motion and tried to send a bullet into Phil Bray, at the cashier's window. But Joe Mantry observed the janitor in plenty of time. Joe was apparently busy only with the stuff he was pulling out of the safe and stuffing into a canvas sack. But he observed Hal Parson in plenty of time, made a fine, snappy draw of his Colt, and dropped Hal with a bullet right through the body.

The janitor fell on the floor and began to kick himself around in a circle and claw at his wounded body with both hands. Joe Mantry, having really seen to the safe pretty thoroughly by this time, snatched up the canvas sack and raced away with it. Bray and Dave Lister backed toward the front door of the bank.

That was when the cashier came to himself. He dropped to his knees behind his wall, grabbed a gun off the lowest shelf, and opened fire just as the robbers leaped out of the front door, and as Rucker came running from his inner office into his ruined bank.

Wayland could not tell whether or not he had succeeded in sending a slug into one of the bandits. They had scattered to either side the instant they got free of the door of the bank.

Wayland got out to the street, and saw that four men, in a scattered line, were riding down the main street as fast as they could drive their horses.

His shouts gave the alarm. The barking of his Colt as he fired after the fugitives helped to call out the men of the town. All up and down the street there were horses standing at various hitch racks, and now men rushed out of doorways and literally vaulted out of windows and flung themselves into saddles.

Still, none of the four fugitives had been knocked from his saddle by the bullets that hailed after them. They swept around the curve of the lower street in a solid body and disappeared from view.

ALL FOR ONE

PHIL BRAY HAD COMMAND, BUT DAVE LISTER KNEW the country better than the others, and therefore he gave advice as to the twist and the turns they had better make when they got back into the mountains.

They were well out from Elkdale, with their horses running well—depending upon Phil Bray to make sure

10

that the horses were as good as money could buy—
when bad luck struck them down. Their horses were
good enough to gain slowly, consistently, on the riders
from the town of Elkdale, but they were not fast enough
to outfoot bad luck.

It came in the form of an old prospector who had a
rifle slung from his shoulder instead of thrust into the
pack of his burro, simply because ten minutes before
this hour he had determined that the time had come
when he must begin to look about him for a little fresh
meat.

He had not seen so much as a rabbit when, looking
down into the valley, he saw a stream of half a hundred
riders raising a dust from the direction of Elkdale, and
far ahead of them there was a quartet of fugitives.

The prospector took them to be fugitives—not the
leaders of a pursuit. And since he was a fellow who
always followed the first thought, and obeyed every
original emotion, he straightway leveled his rifle and
took a crack at the strangers.

It was a six-hundred-yard shot, and he fired just
before the four men got into a pine wood, so he had no
way of knowing what his bullet had accomplished.

As a matter of fact, it had driven into the side of the
horse which rat-faced Jimmy Lovell was riding. His
mount stopped to a stagger, and Jimmy shouted:

"Chief! Lister! Mantry! I'm gone! The mare is dyin'
under me!"

Bray reined up his horse, though Lister said savagely,
curtly:

"We can spare Lovell the best of the lot. Better let
him go than have all of us snagged."

But Bray, swinging in beside Lovell, motioned him to
climb up behind him.

11

"All for one, and one for all!" said Bray.

He had read that in a book—he forgot where—and he liked the sound of it. It had a special meaning for him.

"All for one, and one for all!" he thundered again, and got his horse under way once more.

But in half a mile the extra weight, the up grade, and the approach of sounds of the pursuit from behind them told all four that Bray's horse could carry double no longer.

Mantry was the lightest of the riders, except little Lovell himself. So Mantry took up the handicap, and managed very well with it, because Mantry was a genius when it came to handling horseflesh.

But, inside of another mile or so, Mantry's own horse was stopping to a walk, and the men from Elkdale were thundering along closer.

It was clear that the carrying of Jimmy Lovell might ruin all four of the men. And as Dave Lister took Lovell up behind him in turn, he shouted to Bray:
"Name one of us! Let's make a choice. One of us had better go down than all of us. We're all lost if we try to pack extra weight. We're all done for—and there's a dead man back there in Elkdale! Mantry killed a man for us back there! Think, Phil! It's life or death!"

Phil Bray gripped his horse hard with his knees and rose in the saddle, shouting:

"All for one, and one for all, and damn the traitors what leave a partner in a pinch!"

He added: "Can we duck down one of these side canyons, Dave?"

For narrow ravines branched off on either side from the course of the valley down which the horses were straining.

"Half of 'em are box canyons that'd bring us up agin'

12

a solid wall," answered Lister. "I don't know which are which, but this one oughta be all right!"

He swung to the right as he spoke, and rushed his tiring horse down the canyon. It opened big and wide and deep before them at the start. At the first turning it narrowed. At the next turn they saw before them a fifty-foot wall of almost sheer rock, and over it a thin flag of spray was falling and fanning out into a mist.

That was the prospect before them. Behind them they heard the uproar, as of an advancing sea, when the posse from Elkdale swarmed into the head of the ravine that held them:

They were bottled up. Surrender was all they had before them. And when they surrendered, they could contemplate the death of Hal Parson back there in Elkdale.

Joe Mantry was not the only man who would hang for that murder. The entire quartet would be strung up.

The shrill, piercing voice of Jimmy Lovell was heard yelling: "Lister, you got us into this blind pocket, damn you!"

Lister turned in the saddle and jerked his elbow into the face of Lovell, knocking him headlong from the saddle.

He got up with a great red streak across his features, silenced.

Bray was already climbing the talus of broken rock at the base of the cliff, calling out:

"We'll make a try, boys. There may be a chance here. One for all, all for one!"

They scanned the height and the sheer, glistening face of the cliff with despair, but it was better to try something than to surrender.

Up the talus they ran. Bray, leading, found a way of

13

working up a cleft in the rock to the left that brought them within some seven or eight yards of the top. Farther it was absolutely impossible for any human being to mount the rock.

But Bray shouted: "We'll make a ladder, boys! I'll be the first round. Here, Lister. Climb up over me. Come on, Mantry, and stand on Lister's shoulders. Now, Jimmy Lovell. You don't weigh anything. Up you go, boy. Up like a squirrel. If one of us can get away—and the loot with him—he can buy us out with a smart lawyer, maybe. Up with you!"

They formed the living ladder as their chief commanded.

Bray was the base of it, standing with bent head, submitting to weight after weight as Lister first clambered up and stood on his shoulders. Lister found a handhold on the rock to steady the pile as Joe Mantry in his turn climbed up the ladder and stood on the shoulders of Lister. Last of all came Jimmy Lovely whining, clumsy with fear. And as at last he stood on top of the living ladder, he cried: "I can't reach it!"

"Jump!" commanded Joe Mantry.

"I can't—I'll fall and break my neck," groaned Jimmy Lovell.

"Jump, or I'll throw you down with my own hands!" threatened Joe Mantry.

So threatened, Lovell finally gathered courage enough to leap up. The force with which he sprang nearly tore the clinging fingers of Mantry from the rock. But Lovell had hooked his hands over the upper ledge, and now he scrambled to safety on the ledge above, while a bullet thudded against the cliff close to Phil Bray's face.

Down came Mantry and Dave Lister, while Bray

14

grabbed that precious canvas sack and, with a whirl, hurled it high up into the air, where the hands of Jimmy Lovell reached out. Then Lovell disappeared among the rocks and brush of the upper floor of the valley.

Below came the men of Elkdale, with pale-faced Oliver Wayland riding at the head of them all. He was no expert with horses, but the consuming passion of his shame and his desire to strike one blow on behalf of the bank had brought him finally to the lead. It was his own quick guesswork rather than anything he saw or heard that had led him down this canyon from the main valley; and the rest of the hunt had streaked in behind him.

They saw the canvas sack disappear. They saw the three criminals who were brought to bay stand with their hands raised above their heads in surrender.

Joe Mantry, who saw red when there was a chance to fight, was snarling imprecations and wishing to get at his guns, but Phil Bray had commanded:

"Jimmy Lovell will get us a lawyer who'd argue us out of the gates of hell. Don't go and make a fool of yourself, Joe, and let the rest of us into the hot soup. Take your time."

"Suppose that Lovell decides to forget us and grab that coin for himself?" demanded Joe Mantry.

"He knows the rule of the gang," said Bray. "One for all, and all for one. He won't forget that we carried him along today, and put ourselves into the soup for his sake. He looks like a rat, but he's a man, after all."

That was why they stood there with their hands over their heads, while the men of Elkdale swarmed about them and put the handcuffs over their wrists.

Two thirds of the party followed Wayland when a way had been found so that they could clamber to the upper level of the valley above the cliff. For three days

Wayland hunted through the mountains. But he did not even know the face of the man he was pursuing. He merely had vague ideas about the build of him. The rest of the men from Elkdale gave up the chase, and at last Wayland himself surrendered the hunt and came gloomily back to Elkdale.

There he found the doors of the bank closed, and the significant sign which he had known he would find was posted over the doors.

Unshaven, haggard, he went to the house of Rucker. The banker himself, almost as unkempt as his cashier, opened the door and stood staring at him with a frozen face.

"Well," said Wayland foolishly, "I didn't catch him."

"No?" said Rucker, and a sardonic smile pulled at his lips.

He kept his hand on the door, blocking the way, staring.

"I suppose you're through with me?" asked Wayland.

Rucker smiled again.

And as the world spun about before the eyes of Wayland, he asked:

"Can I see May?"

After a moment, still blocking the way, Rucker turned his head and called out:

"May!"

A voice answered far off. Footsteps came hurrying. A door opened, and there she was, moving through the dimness of the hall.

"Here's Wayland, wanting to know if he can see you," said Rucker.

The girl halted. Like her father, she said nothing. She was white. In the dark of the hallway it seemed to Wayland that the white of her face was like a pearl

16

shining against black velvet.

The silence held for a frightful moment, and then Rucker slammed the door in Wayland's face.

He turned and went down the steps to the street. It was not empty. Children were playing half a block away, running through the dust and yelling and laughing. In the solemn chamber of his soul the voices echoed mournfully.

It was a good, brisk trial. The evidence was all there, laid out smoothly. But Wayland was not attending the sessions of the court. He was sitting in the little one-story hospital at the edge of the town, tending to Hal Parson, who was dying. The doctors had said that Parson could not live a day. He ended by living ten. But he could not eat. And gradually the strength went out of him.

He endured a constant agony with wonderful courage. He seemed to have only one regret.

"I let you down," he said to Wayland. "If I hadn't been slowed up with the booze, I would 'a' got that gun out and plastered one of the thugs. Maybe I would 'a' got the whole gang of 'em on the run. You can't tell. But I fell down on you after you trusted me!"

"If I'd put up a man's fight," Wayland told him, "there wouldn't have been a need of you. I'm not a man. I'm a yellow dog. That's all!"

"You?" said Hal Parson. He tried to laugh, but the pain stopped him. "You're a better man than you know your own self," he managed to gasp at last.

Ten days after the robbery they buried Hal Parson.

Rucker came to the funeral, and May Rucker brought flowers for the grave. Neither she nor her father would look at the white, drawn face of Wayland, who had arranged everything.

He saw the earth heaped over the grave, and then stalked back into the town to the courtroom, where he could barely find standing room to squeeze himself in. He heard the last of the evidence. He heard the faltering, rather casual appeal of the lawyer who had been appointed by the judge to defend the criminals. The result was a foregone conclusion.

For Jimmy Lovell, after all, had proved himself more of a rat than he was a man; he had not come to the aid of his friends in need as they had come to his.

Wayland, standing with a cold stone for a heart, saw the judge put on the black cap, heard him pronounce the words, "To be hanged by the neck until you are dead, dead, dead!"

All three of the men were to hang. That made little difference to Wayland. It seemed to him as though he were himself already dead and ready for the grave.

IN THE DEATH HOUSE

THE DEATH HOUSE IN THE ATWATER PRISON SHOULD be celebrated for its view. It stands above the rest of the building, rising like a tower between the inner and the outer yard. The windows peer down on the outer walls and look beyond them at the Ballater Mountains. That being the southeastern face of the Ballater Mountains, there isn't a tree or a shrub in sight; they are nothing but wind-sculptured rock whose flutings and hollows are painted blue, or brown, or rosy-gold, according to the time of day. There is a moment before noon where hardly a shadow is seen, for the sun strikes right against the average slope of the range and sets the crystals of the granite gleaming like intolerably bright little stars.

The beauty of the mountains was generally unnoticed by the men who were spending time in the death house, but on this occasion one of the prisoners was an æsthete who could not overlook scenery. As the evening crept up from the plain like water, submerging the feet of the peaks, Dave Lister had summoned his companions. They crowded their heads beside his in order to look out through the little barred window.

"A perfect picture, and a perfect evening to remember this earth by," said Dave Lister. "I hope you fellows will appreciate it."

Joe Mantry, the jokester, and Phil Bray, the leader, looked grimly on their companion. The three should not have been permitted to occupy one cell, but Jefferson Bergman, the warden, knew that no man had ever escaped from the death house, and it seemed pretty apparent that no man ever *would* escape. So the warden decided to reward these three for the unanimity of mind and the resolution of spirit with which they had stood together during the chase in which they had been captured, and the trial in which they had perjured themselves with a perfect singleness of heart. Since they were to hang at dawn, Jefferson Bergman was pleased to allow them to spend the last night of their lives in the same cell in the death house. That was the reason they were able to crowd their heads together at one window and listen to the slow, emotional voice of David Lister.

Joe Mantry laughed.

"Are you going to enjoy the scenery we'll have in hell?" he asked. "Are you going to call us to admire down there, Dave?"

Phil Bray did not laugh. He never laughed. But his big mouth stretched a little in a grin.

"No matter what the scenery is," he said, "we're

19

going, to have a chance to enjoy it together."

"To the devil with the mountains, and let's get back to seven-up," said Joe Mantry. He was handsome, and dark, and slender, and a little too sleek. "But why," he added, "d'you think that we'll all stick together in hell? Won't we be shuffled apart?"

"They can't," said Phil Bray. "Even in hell they can't pry partners loose."

Dave Lister had gone back to his end of the table, where he was writing his last words with careful phraseology and with a still more careful pen. Dave was a forger of note, and he had selected as his hand for these last important words, the exact script of a celebrated traveler, millionaire, and poet whose handwriting Dave had studied long ago, and not in vain. That study had enabled Dave Lister to cash several important checks in the past; now it was permitting him to express himself in the strong, flowing characters of a poet of some note. But he suspended his pen above the paper and ran his pale fingers through the silken length of his hair while he answered the last remark.

"Yes," he said, "we'll all be together in hell. Each of us is just as bad as the other. We weigh the same, and we'll sink to the same level."

"No," said Phil Bray. "The kid, here, don't belong with us. He ain't done much. He's only been careless."

Dave Lister tilted back his head and half closed his eyes.

"Joseph Mantry," he said, "the murderer? Careless? How many men have you killed, Joe?"

"Aw, shut up," said Mantry.

"Twenty-one years old. Seven dead men behind him. Yes, he's been a little careless. Just a little careless. Matter of fact, you've never been happy except when you were careless, Joe. Am I right about that?"

"I got a mind to sock you on the chin," said Joe Mantry.

Dave Lister caressed his long, pointed, fragile chin. He smiled at Mantry.

"That's all right, boy," he said.

"But count the chief out," said Mantry. "Phil looks hard, but he's got a heart as big as a mountain."

"Of course he has," said Lister, "and made of what makes mountains, too. Rock! Phil Bray is a lion; you're a murdering fox, Joe."

"And what about yourself?" asked Mantry.

"I'm a snake," said Lister.

"Yeah, with a lot of poison in your tooth, too,"accused Mantry.

"Of course," said Lister, growing absent-minded "Of course, plenty of poison."

He turned his attention to his writing, doing a word at a time, sprawling out the, letters with a fine dash and flourish, and then pausing until he had the next word in mind and had moved his pen for a moment in the air in order to prepare his hand for the next stroke on the paper.

He continued to write for some time, while Joe Mantry, growing tired of the card game, pushed back his chair, left the table, and sauntered to the bars of the cell. Two guards were on duty in the corridor. Mantry said:

"Hello, Bill. Want a drink?"

The three had asked for whisky for their last night, and they had two bottles of it at hand.

Bill licked his lips, started to rise from his chair, and then slumped back into it. He shook his head.

"You know I can't take a shot while I'm on the job,"

21

he said.

"I'm sorry," said Joe. "I'd like to have a drink with you, Bill, and talk about your family."

"You know my family?" asked Bill innocently.

"Sure," said Joe Mantry. "I met your father in New York, where he was shoveling coal with a lot of other cross-eyed dumb-bells, and I saw your greaser mother down in Mexico City, where she was scrubbing floors on her hands and knees."

Bill got up from his chair with a howl of anger.

"Joe!" called Philip Bray. "Quit it!"

"Aw, all right, all right," said Joe Mantry. He turned his reckless head toward Bray. "Why can't you leave me alone while I stir up this blockhead?"

"It's because of Jeff Bergman," said Phil Bray. "He's given us a break, letting us spend the last night together. If you start a brawl up here, you're double-crossing him. What good would it do? There ain't any use double-crossing a bird unless you can get something out of it."

Joe Mantry listened to this bit of philosophizing with a grin. He cast a lingering glance toward Bill, the guard, who was still cursing, and then shrugged his shoulders.

"All right, Phil," said Mantry. "But I'm tired of cards. Tell me a story to pass the time of day, will you?"

"Sure," said Phil Bray, nodding. "What kind of a story?"

"A fairy story."

"Good fairies or bad?" asked Bray, grinning.

"Good fairies. That's the kind I need just now. Tell me a story about Jim Silver and Parade."

"I never seen him," said Bray. "What would a mug like me get out of Jim Silver except a rap on the chin or a chunk of lead through the bean?"

"Look, Phil," said Joe Mantry; "you're a handy gent

22

with your hands. You got plenty of size and plenty of nerve, and you know the game. Would you be scared of big Jim Silver if you got into a fist fight with him? I mean, suppose guns was barred, would you be scared of him?"

"I remember a gent by name of Cyclone Ed Guerney," said Phil Bray. "The Cyclone was two hundred and twenty, and all of it mean. He was right in there with the best of 'em, and only the booze parted him from the headliners in the end. But Cyclone Ed got himself back into training to take a crack at Jim Silver with his fists, and when he was in good shape again, and could do an hour of shadow boxing and still breathe clean, he picked on Jim Silver one day."

The voice of Bray died out, and his eyes grew reminiscent.

"Go on," said Mantry.

"Well," said Bray. "I seen Cyclone Guerney about a month afterward, and he still couldn't talk except out of one corner of his mouth. The cuts had healed up a good deal, and the bruises was just pale-green. But he didn't look nacheral."

"Had he done anything to Silver in the scrap?" asked Mantry curiously.

"Cyclone Ed told me that socking at Silver was like punching at a shadow, and every time Silver hit him it was like being slapped with the butt end of a blacksnake."

"What does this bird Silver get out of his game?" demanded Mantry. "Where does he pull down the long green?"

"It ain't the cash that he wants. It's the fun. His idea of a good time is finding a hard nut and cracking it. That's all."

"Why don't he get a job as a sheriff, then?"

"He'd have to stay put in one place. And he likes to keep on moving."

Mantry yawned.

"To the devil with Silver and all the other funny birds," said he. "Dave, what you writing?"

"I'm writing," said Lister solemnly, "the whole truth about Jimmy Lovell and how he double-crossed us and let us down—the dirty dog! I got it written up to the point where we were cornered, and no way out, and how the three of us made a living ladder up the rock, and how Jimmy climbed up over us and got away."

"Wait a minute," commanded Bray. "Lemme see that."

He took the sheet of paper and glanced over the contents. Then he tore it up, rending it to small bits, in spite of Lister's angry protest.

The heap of fragments Bray put into a saucer, lighted them, and watched them throw up a strong flame and then a cloud of smoke.

"There's a couple of hours of work in that job!" exclaimed Lister. "What's the matter with you, Phil?"

"We ain't going to put the police on Jimmy Lovell," said Bray. "It wouldn't be right."

"You mean to let him get away with the loot while we go to hell?" demanded Lister.

"I don't know," muttered Bray. "All I know is that if we can't get our hands on him, we ain't going to let anybody else have the pleasure. They wouldn't do a job. They wouldn't do a good job, And it's better not to start on Jimmy Lovell at all unless he can be finished the way that we would finish."

"Here's the warden," said Mantry.

The door at the end of the corridor opened, and big Jefferson Bergman walked in.

24

WAYLAND'S OFFER

BERGMAN LOVED THAT PRISON, AND HAD WORKED HIS way up from the bottom of the ladder. He had begun by scrubbing floors, advanced to the proud uniform of a guard, distinguished himself in stopping two jail breaks, and finally had been appointed warden. He wore the signs of his stormy years in his battered face. He was a big fellow, with a bullet head which he kept closely clipped, so that one could see the large, fat wrinkles bulging above his neck and over the base of his skull.

As he came in, he waved to the guards.

"You can go off duty for an hour, boys," he said. "Go and stretch your legs. I'll keep an eye on the lads."

"I'm glad to be off the job," said Bill. "That bird Mantry, I wanta sock him in the eye."

The guards left.

As the two passed off duty, through the door came the tall form and the pale face of Wayland. He stood back, as though not wishing to speak or interfere in any way until he had received express permission from the warden.

"What's the matter between you and Bill?" asked the warden, standing in front of the cell and taking out a cigar. He began to teeter back and forth in his big, square-toed shoes. They were well polished, but the leather was so soft that the brightness of the surface was spoiled by a thousand intercrossing wrinkles. "You boys oughta all be friends," added the warden.

"I just thought that Bill looked like a cross between a greaser and a dumb-bell," said Mantry, grinning, "and so I told him that I'd seen his ma and pa, and what they looked like."

The warden chuckled.

"Here's a fellow that thinks he's got something to say to you men," said the warden. "Step up, Wayland. Talk to 'em. I won't interfere. Step right up to the bars and talk. I'll wait over in the corner, and I won't listen in. I guess you won't be pulling the bars apart to let the gang out."

He chuckled again, and paced over to a corner of the corridor, while Oliver Wayland stepped up before the bars of the cell and looked at the three.

The criminals stared with suddenly interested eyes upon this man. They could remember how he had stood in the bank, with his arms stretched up past his white face. He was nearly as pale now, but there was a firmness of resolution about him that was new.

Men who handle weapons know that there is courage of another sort than that which leads to the shooting of bullets or the wielding of knives. Perhaps there was this other courage, this moral strength, in the ex-cashier.

"You're the chief, Bray," he said. "I want to talk with you."

"Fire away," said Bray, and he came in turn close to the bars.

"Bray," said Wayland, "we know that none of you fellows have any part of the half million that was stolen from the bank. We know that you had a fourth partner who got away with the loot. And we've an idea that you're not too fond of him."

"Have you got that idea?" asked Bray, his upper lip lifting a little. "What give it to you?"

"You didn't have a penny to fight your case for you," said Wayland. "You gave your friend a chance to get away with the cash, and apparently he didn't try to get in touch with a lawyer and buy him up to help you

26

afterward. He simply lay low to take the coin and let you hang."

"You talk like a gent with sense," said Bray. "You talk like you'd gone through the first grade, or something."

"Well," said Wayland, "I didn't come here to waste words on you. I came to offer you a chance for your lives. The law doesn't know the name of your fourth partner. It doesn't even know, very well, what he looks like. And it wants to find out. The only way it can find out is through you men. Will you talk?"

Dave Lister came close and said:

"What would we get out of it? Clean free of jail?"

Oliver Wayland hesitated. "No," he said at last. "Not clean free of jail. But you'd get a change of sentence. A new trial, and something less than life imprisonment. I don't know exactly. But I've talked with some people high up, and they say that it can be managed. Will you talk?"

"You're damn right we'll talk!" said Lister. "We'll tell you his name, what he looks like, and where he hangs out. Is that enough?"

"Plenty!" said Wayland. "And if—"

"Lister is joking," said Bray.

"Joking?" said Lister, with amazement, "when we got a chance—"

"A chance to whine and howl, eh? A chance to turn State's evidence, Dave? Is that what you call a chance?" demanded Bray suddenly.

Lister gaped.

"Joe," he appealed to Mantry. "Here's where we could maybe change to a—"

"Aw, shut up," said Joe Mantry, shrugging his sleek shoulders. "The chief knows what's right, and he knows

27

what's wrong. Leave it to him."

He added: "He has to hang with us, don't he?"

This last argument seemed to be so final and convincing that even Lister was silenced.

Wayland said: "You boys can't turn down an opportunity like this. You can't do it! I'm not talking through my hat. Speak up now, and by midnight I'll be in touch with people who are close to the governor. You'll have a stay of execution before morning. Otherwise—" He made a gesture with his hand.

"Otherwise," completed Bray, "we go to hell, eh?"

"You do," agreed Wayland. "And you leave a traitor to enjoy the half million that you fellows worked to get. You took the main chances. I didn't even see a fourth man until you were all riding down the street."

"Outside jobs and inside jobs," said Bray philosophically, "have to have gents workin' on 'em. That fourth gent had the easy break at the work. He had the easy break when we made the get-away—the rest of us could be free, by this time, while *he* was waiting to have his neck stretched. But that don't make us talk now!"

"Why not?" asked Wayland.

"What he'd get from the law wouldn't be enough to please us. I never gave a damn for what law courts could do. I wouldn't have them work on that skunk in my place right now. That's what we all feel. So long, brother!"

Wayland gave Bray one desperate look, but Bray was set as iron. Lister looked despondent, Mantry indifferent.

"I give up," said Wayland suddenly to the warden. And he walked out down the corridor.

The warden, as the door closed, clipped his cigar with

28

a little gold cigar cutter which had been given to him by the prison staff. When he dropped it back into his coat pocket, it clinked against a heavy bunch of keys.

Phil Bray, hearing that sound, half closed his eyes and looked far away among the shadows of his own mind. He had a pleased expression, as of one who is listening to good music and knows that the best part of the piece is still to be played.

The warden lighted his cigar, tossing his head a little as he puffed out the first heavy clouds. He coughed. Thin blue smoke exploded from, his lips. He wiped a speck of tobacco from his mouth with the red tip of his tongue.

"You fellows got everything you want?" he asked.

"Mostly everything," said young Joe Mantry.

"Except one of those cigars," remarked Phil Bray.

The warden opened his eyes a little. He was inclined to be angry because of the impertinence. These were his own cigars, and he valued them as treasures. But he remembered that men in the death house are supposed to have every wish gratified; it was his own fault if he had come up here and breathed the smoke of a good Havana into the faces of the prisoners.

"All right, Bray," he said. "Here you are."

He pulled one of, the Havanas from his pocket and stepped right in toward the bars. Only at the last instant he saw what was coming, and tried to jerk his head away, but it was too late.

Phil Bray had driven his fist, straight and true, right between two of the bars, and now the weight of it lodged on the point of the warden's chin.

Jefferson Bergman threw his hand over his head and fell on his back. Then he began to stir a little, moving slightly from side to side.

29

None of the prisoners spoke. They understood the plan of Phil Bray before a word of it had been uttered. Now they reached through the bars and tried to catch hold of the leg and the foot of Bergman that was nearer to the cell.

Bray and Mantry could not get a grip, but the long arm of the penman enabled him to get his clutch on the flap of the trouser leg. He closed his fingers like the talons of a bird. Then, pulling back, he swayed the leg in toward the cell.

Instantly Bergman kicked himself free!

He got to his feet with a groan and an oath. He had a gun in his right hand now. The good Havana had been smashed, and the cinders had burned and blackened all one side of his face, yet he still kept the cigar well gripped between his teeth.

He cursed as he swayed to his feet. It had been a double shock—the fist against his jaw and the back of his head against the floor. The result was that when he regained his feet he stumbled suddenly forward toward the bars of the cell.

Bray was not quick enough to seize the opportunity. Perhaps he was not quite swift enough in his reactions to take advantage of the chance. But the long, skinny arms of the penman plunged through between the bars at once. He caught Bergman by the coat collar, jerked him violently forward, and crashed his forehead firmly against a steel bar.

The revolver slid down his trouser leg and clinked against the floor.

Bergman stood with staring, idiotic eyes. He put out one hand and took a mild grip on the bars. And the penman, a whine of impatient and savage joy in his throat, beat the head of the warden again and again against the bars.

They cut the flesh right through to the bone. Blood gushed down the face of the warden. Horrible wounds multiplied. His knees had buckled. But the frenzy of Dave Lister gave him strength to hold up the loose, bulky weight and still crash the head of Bergman against the bars.

At last the burden slid out of his numb finger tips.

He stood there gasping, shaking, looking down at his hands. Blood was spattered over his fingers, and smeared over the sleeves of his coat.

"That was a good one," said Phil Bray. "I guess you cooked the poor bum, Dave. Got 'em, Joe?"

Joe Mantry's hand was fumbling in the coat pocket of the warden. He found the keys, jumped up with them, and, reaching his hand through the bars of the door, started trying keys in the lock.

Phil Bray went back to the table, poured out a good shot of whisky, and let it run slowly down his throat.

"I was just thinking," he said in a meditative voice. "What you suppose that Jimmy Lovell could feel like if he could see what we're doin' now?"

The penman stared at his chief.

"You're as cool as anything," he declared. "I don't care what Jimmy would feel like. I know what I'll feel like once I get on the outside of the guard wall."

"Sure," agreed Bray.

"They won't get us alive the next time," said Dave Lister, trembling from head to foot.

"Sure they won't. They won't get us at all," answered the chief.

"Take those keys yourself—lemme take 'em—Joe's wasting time—and they're coming! The guard's coming back," breathed Lister.

"Easy, Dave" said the chief. "We don't know nothing about locks—not compared with Mantry. We ain't got no fingers—not compared with him."

Something clicked softly. The door of the, cell opened, and the three, lost in a moment of panic and joy that carried even big Phil Bray away with the enthusiasm, rushed out into the corridor.

They were still far from freedom, but this first step seemed half of the distance.

What should they do next?

There were two revolvers—one in the coat of the warden and the other which had slid from his hand to the floor. Bray took one of them. The penman took the other, cursed, and reluctantly passed it across to Joe Mantry, as to a greater genius with firearms.

He said to Joe: "You know me, kid."

"Yeah. You'll get a pill before I do, if the pinch comes," said Mantry.

They had agreed through the mere interchange of mute glances that they would not be taken. If it came to the final stand and shooting, they would save three bullets for themselves.

"You're the best doctor. See if the warden's dead, Dave," ordered Bray.

So Dave kneeled beside the warden and put his ear over the heart of the big fellow.

"Dead," he said. "I must 'a' bashed in his skull for him. Now what?"

"That's the right double cross," said Mantry to the chief.

"Yeah," said big Phil Bray. "That's a double cross that done us some good. How do we get out of here? If we go down the stairs, we're sure to bump into some-body."

"Yeah. Try the back door of the death house, and then over the roof. When we done our last turn in the yard I seen a ladder against the west side."

"I remember. Where the masons got their scaffolding," said Bray to this suggestion from Mantry. "But they'd take the ladder down by night."

"They wouldn't," said Mantry. "They wouldn't take it down. Because that's our only chance."

They looked at one another for a split part of a second. Then Bray said:

"All right, Joe. Try the back door."

It stood at the farther end of the corridor. Mantry found the right key for it almost at once, and they slipped through the door onto the roof. It was almost flat. A little distance away that roof dropped two stories to the level of the rest of the building. They could see three walls of the prison in part. On those, to the south and east they could see the sentinels walking their beats. They could see the gleam of the rifles. Beyond the walls were the guardhouses, the little circular redoubts, with strong searchlights mounted in the top of each, throwing sweeping rays over the blackness of the ground.

How could a man do anything unseen?

Well, they were to die in the morning, anyway.

Bray ran back to the cell, got two blankets from a cot, and came out again, knotting the corners of the blankets together. That made a rope of some length. They hurried out to the edge of the roof, crawling. A strong drain projected. Bray tied an end of the blanket rope to the drain and let the rest of the length dangle. It came about eight or nine feet short of the roof beneath. A wind was blowing. It fanned the blanket out and swung it to the side across the field of one of the little barred windows.

Behind that window was some fellow who called

33

himself unlucky—some one who had a little stretch, a fiver or so, to do. A fellow who wasn't due to die in the morning, who didn't have to come out by night and try to run the impossible gantlet of the walls, the guards, the guardhouses beyond the walls.

The three had their shoes off by this time, and Bray went down first. The others followed. It was not a very jarring drop to the roof below. So they left the blanket dangling, hanging like a limp, pale-gray flag to attract attention. Then they stole across the roof to the place where the scaffold for the masons and the ladder had been placed that day.

The scaffold was gone, and the ladder lay flat in the yard far below!

ON THE ROOF

THERE WAS A NEST OF THREE CHIMNEYS THAT ROSE IN a close cluster out of the slope of the roof near the side of the prison. The fugitives took shelter there. The greatness of their danger made them small as insects. The guards that could be seen striding along the guard walks on the southern and eastern walls were great giants. Sometimes as the guards came to the end of their beats, they would speak for a moment with the relief sentinels who kept post in the little towers that were placed here and there on the walls. In each of those towers there were two machine guns. One pointed in on the prison yard, and one swept the country beyond the walls. The men who worked those machine guns had to practice constantly. They knew the exact range of every spot of ground beyond point-blank. They were experts.

The staggering whisper of the penman said: "I seen

the bodies of Flaherty and Coons. They were cut in two. They were ripped right in two, the pair of them. That's how close the bullets out of that machine gun come together."

"Wait'll we get far enough to have the machine guns open up on us," said Phil Bray. "There ain't any sense being afraid of things that we ain't reached yet."

He sat up and looked around him. The stars swarmed lower in the sky in shining clusters. Time went by rapidly. The stars drifted up in the east and drifted down in the west. The wheel of the constellations was turning. It seemed to be spinning with an increasing speed.

That was because in time the wheel would turn the sun up above the eastern horizon. When that happened, the men would come to the death house. They would see the warden lying on the floor, dead. They would see the empty cell.

No, long before that they would discover the break. The two guards would return at the end of one hour. And was not that hour almost ended now?

Bray sat up, his head tilted back at a sharp angle, a strangling angle. He had a magnificent face. He would have been more handsome than Joe Mantry, even, had it not been that his nose was too small. It by no means filled up the space that extended between mouth and brow. It gave one a sense of emptiness among the features. One sees that emptiness most often in the, face of an ape.

"We gotta go back," Bray said.

"We gotta go where?" said Dave Lister. "Go back to the cell, you mean? *You* go back if you want to. I ain't such a fool. I'd rather go to hell."

"We gotta go back," said Bray.

"All right, baby," answered Joe Mantry. "You go

back, and I'll stay here and be a rear guard."

"We gotta go back," said Bray.

"You go back then," said Dave Lister. "I'll stay here. When they find us, we dive off the edge of the roof. That's all right. Or else we just sit still and plug ourselves. We got the guns to do it. Out here we can pick and choose."

"Maybe we can pick and choose some of the guards when it gets light enough," remarked Joe Mantry. "I'd like to get me the big freckle-faced son that kicked me in the ribs that day. Maybe I'll get a chance at him before they turn the lights on the roof. Maybe he'll come out here to hunt for us. Would I laugh if I got a chance to unload a few slugs into him?"

"We gotta go back," said Phil Bray.

He crawled straight out from among the chimney pots. Dave Lister clung to his coat tails, whispering: "Don't go, chief. They'll see you. They'll give you away. What are you doing to us?"

Bray struck the hand of Lister away and went on. Joe Mantry crawled out in pursuit.

"We gotta go with the chief," he whispered to Lister.

"Yeah, we gotta go—with him!" panted the penman, and took up his own way across the roof.

They got to the place where the blanket rope hung down from the drain pipe two stories up. Instantly they made a human ladder: Bray was the foundation of it. Lister climbed over him, and then helped Mantry up with a swing that took him well on his way, and in a moment Joe Mantry was sprawling out on the top of the roof above. The tall, thin-legged body of Dave Lister followed. Phil Bray, himself had to run back and then sprint forward and leap high in his stockinged feet before he managed to catch the end of the blanket rope.

36

But his grip was strong, and he handed himself up the length of the blankets until he was with his friends above.

There he stretched out, panting.

For Dave Lister had gasped: "The east guard has spotted us! Flatten out, boys!"

They pressed themselves out on the roof. The guard who walked the eastern wall had, in fact, halted in his pacing, and was looking directly toward them, as it seemed: The signal would be three rapid shots from his rifle. That signal would start the alarm bell clanging. Every guard in the prison would come to life with a jump.

The rifle shots were not fired. The guard continued to pace the wall. Phil Bray led the way back through the unlocked door at the end of the death house. As he crawled through and rose to his feet, he remained for a moment bent forward, as though he were dodging a blow.

"The warden!" he gasped. "Boys, the warden's body is gone!"

"Are dead men walking tonight?" breathed Dave Lister.

The three of them crowded around the spot where the warden had lain. There was a big pool of blood about the smudged outline which the head and shoulders of poor Bergman had left on the concrete floor. A good quart of blood seemed to have spilled out there in an irregular splotch such as a hurled egg would leave on a wall. Only at one point the red liquid had flowed away in a long stream.

"Who's been in here? Who's carried him out? Why ain't the alarm bell ringing?" demanded Phil Bray.

"The alarm will start in a minute," answered Joe

Mantry. "And then the music will start. Well, there's enough food left up here to keep us going for two or three days—booze, too—and we've got enough bullets in here to keep them backed up. Why, boys, this is going to be a party!"

"We're going on from here," said Phil Bray. "Maybe we've still got a chance!"

He opened the door which commanded the head of the stairs. Those steps went down to a landing where a bright light was burning. There was another powerful lamp burning just above the door which Bray had opened. A funnel of brightness seemed to be pouring up into his face; the law was laying a ghostly hand on him, thrusting him back.

"Come here, Joe!" he commanded.

Joe Mantry approached, saying: "It's better this way. We'll have, a couple of days; that's better than a couple of hours!"

"Shut up, you fool! They'd smoke us out in a few minutes," answered Phil Bray. "Climb up on my shoulder and jimmy that electric light, will you? Maybe the other stairway lights work on the same switch. Maybe we can blow the lot of 'em! And if —"

Joe Mantry leaped at him with a grunt of eagerness. It was perfectly apparent that if the stairs could be buried in darkness, the three of them would be able to take at least a few long steps in the direction of freedom. Joe Mantry stood up, like the sure-footed athlete that he was, on the shoulders of his chief. He rose on tiptoes, reached the electric bulb, and turned it out. In another moment, with his Colt, he had "jimmied" the fixture. There was a faint snapping, hissing sound, and the flash of a spark; afterward there was thick darkness on the landing of the stairs below them.

"Now, boys!" said Phil Bray, and Mantry dropped down again.

Their unshod feet made rapid whispering, thumping sounds as they fled down the stairs. Suddenly some one began to shout far before them, demanding light, cursing.

They turned around the corner of the stairs, and heard the voice immediately in front of them. They ran it down. The butt of Bray's gun struck down the clamorer. The man fell with a long groan, and tumbled down half a dozen steps.

Other voices began to shout. Light glimmered over the stairs at the next landing. They stole into the field of it like three guilty shadows. People were speaking excitedly. One man was shouting:

"Listen, chief! Tell us what happened! Who did it? Did you fall down? What happened?"

"He's dying! He's been brained!" shouted another. "Speak to us, chief!"

Off that landing place, double doors opened upon a corridor of a cell room, and there the three criminals saw the warden standing with blood running down his hideous face, and wide-open, staring eyes that saw nothing, while two of his assistants gripped his arms, supporting his staggering body and trying to get speech out of him.

The warden, as the three forms slipped out of darkness, across the landing, and down the next flight of the stairs, slowly raised his hand and pointed after them. Dave Lister, last of the three, distinctly saw the gesture!

THE ALARM

DOWN THE STAIRS WENT THE THREE—ANOTHER flight, and another—and in the lower hall they heard voices exclaiming loudly.

"The warden'll have his wits back in a minute—and he saw us all go by—if he can talk to 'em!" breathed Dave Lister. "Quick, Joe! Oh, quick!"

Joe Mantry already had found the lock of the door in the darkness. He had selected, with his sure, slim fingers, the largest of the keys. Now he slid it home in the lock and turned.

Some one was saying: "Here—here's the lantern at last!"

Suddenly waves of lantern light washed through the hall, all down the length of it. Dave Lister, as usual, was the one of the three who looked back. He made out three or four dark forms halfway down the hall. He saw a man coming at a run, a lantern swinging crazily in his hand.

Then Joe Mantry opened the door, and they leaped outside and closed the door behind them.

The prison yard—the outer yard—was empty. Not a soul stirred in it. And the guard on the southern wall, , looking gigantic against the stars, was walking away from them. His rifle wavered with a dim gleam as he carried it on his shoulder.

They turned the corner of the prison building, following after Phil Bray, and since they were now in front of the main structure, the gate of the guard wall was straight ahead of them. Toward that went Phil Bray, with his stocking-footed companions closing up beside him.

40

"We'll put a gun on the gatekeeper. We'll make him open up for us," said Phil Bray softly. "No crazy work, now. You, Dave—you keep hold of yourself!"

"Like steel!" whispered Dave Lister. "Like steel!" He kept saying that over and over, his voice hissing against his teeth:

"Like steel! Like steel!"

Dave was the weak link in the chain of three. If he held, all might go well.

The gatehouse was a little sentry box beside the huge double door that came together to close the entrance to the prison. In the face of that box there was a little oval window with a light behind it, and when Bray glanced inside he saw the gatekeeper sitting with his visored, official cap pushed halfway back on his head. He wore a blue coat with brass buttons; his stomach puffed out against the serge in a great double fold.

Bray pushed open the narrow door at the side and slid his revolver under the nose of the gatekeeper. There was blood on the gun and blood on the hand of Bray.

"All right, brother," he said. "Open up for us!"

The gatekeeper kept on looking at the gun. All the color about his mouth disappeared. His lips were the color of gray stone, and, like stone, they seemed incapable of uttering speech. His mouth fell open and left his chin resting on his breast.

Joe Mantry glided in beside him, jerked a revolver out of the holster at the guard's hip, and tapped him lightly over the head with the barrel of it. The cap fell off and exposed silver-gray hair, with the pink sheen of the scalp through the thinness of it.

"Start moving, grandpa!" said Mantry.

The gatekeeper got up, using more the force of his arms than the strength of his legs.

41

"The three of them!" he muttered. "The three of them!"

He pulled out a drawer of the little desk before him, and took out three keys for the three great locks of the gate. Then he walked outside with the three behind him, shouldering him with their closeness.

"Keep the guns out of sight. Don't let 'em shine!" whispered Bray.

They kept the guns out of sight, but they kept them pointing at the gatekeeper. There was a weapon for each of them now. The thin fingers of Dave Lister kept gripping and relaxing on the handle of his newly acquired Colt.

"Hey, Joe!" called a voice from the wall above. "Hey, Joe, all right?"

Out of the little guard tower above, to the side of the gate, a man was leaning, peering down.

"Answer!" said Bray, giving the gatekeeper his knee.

"Hi!" exclaimed the gatekeeper in a vague, bawling voice.

"What's that?" called the guard above them.

"It's all right!" whispered Bray. "Say that, or else "

"It's all right!" shouted Joe, the gatekeeper.

He thrust the big keys one by one into the locks. He turned them. And as the second bolt slid back with a dim, clicking sound, the alarm bell suddenly started crashing out of the central sky, pouring brazen ruin about the ears of the fugitives.

"They've got you! Give it tip!" snarled the gatekeeper.

The quick hand of Joe Mantry went past him, turned the third key, and the gate gave way, yawning open slowly.

Tall Dave Lister was the first through the opening.

The noise of the alarm bell had maddened him. He was no longer saying to himself that he must be as cool and strong as steel. He went through that open gate with a bound like a deer and sprinted up the slope straight ahead of him. It made no difference to the madness of Dave Lister that the guard tower on the hill was directly in his path. He was blind. He simply wanted distance between him and the dreadful, irregular pulsation of that bell.

Phil Bray might have killed Joe, the gatekeeper, to make sure that one less enemy was left behind him, but Bray hated blood when he could avoid the shedding of it. He simply gave the man the weight of the butt of his gun under the ear as he went through the gate, and Joe sat down with a sudden thud on the threshold.

"Let Lister go—the fool is ruining us by running!" growled Mantry at the ear of Bray.

"Where one goes, we all go," answered Bray through his teeth. "Come on! We don't welch!"

He charged right up the hill behind Lister. It was gallant; it was true and faithful companionship; but it was also throwing themselves away, perhaps. For an instant Joe Mantry wavered. But he was accustomed to following Bray. And now the force of a superior resolution drew him after his leader once more. He sprinted swiftly on Bray's heels. The long legs of Lister were bounding over the ground well in the lead.

"Who's there? Who's there?" yelled the voice of the guard from above the gate. His words sounded vaguely and largely in the air, half lost in the frightful outcry of the alarm bell. The circling searchlight of the tower on the hill just before them cut across their path, picking them brightly out of the dark of the night.

The guard on the wall started firing.

At the second report of the rifle, Lister leaped into the air with a yell of pain, but landed, running faster than ever.

However, that guard was shooting too straight for comfort. And in another moment the searchlights might light up his target for him.

Phil Bray halted, turned, and took time for one breath to steady himself. Then he fired. He was fifty yards away, and it was a snap shot, but he got the guard right through the hips. The poor fellow folded up, and Bray ran on.

He turned into a greater peril than that from the guards on the prison wall.

The searchlight had snapped across them. Now it returned, letting its big white hand waver over the ground here and there, until it found them once more. It settled on them with a shudder, and then with a steady streaming of illumination. Instinctively the three fanned out to either side to try to get out of that deadly brightness.

Bullets would hail instantly down the path of the searchlight, of course. Even if they succeeded in running past the place, each of these guard towers had fast horses constantly under the saddle, ready to take up a pursuit.

"Shoot for the light!" yelled Bray, setting the example as he ran.

But the gun kept jumping falsely in his hand. Bullets began to whine through the air about him, while the madman, Dave Lister, still ran right on into the white light to ruin.

He was not even using his gun, however blindly.

But Joe Mantry was shooting, firing just as his left foot parted from the ground each time. With his second shot he smashed the fragile mechanism of the searchlight. There was a crunching and then a tinkling fall of broken glass.

Tall Dave Lister, well in the lead of the other two, rounded the side of the little guard tower.

His two companions could see what happened. The horses were there, tied to a rack, looking like angels of promise to those panting runners. As Lister sprang for the rack, the rear door of the guard tower opened.

Lister fired twice. The door slammed shut, and there was a wild howling of pain from inside the little building.

Joe Mantry and his chief hit the saddle leather not a second behind Lister.

Out of the rear window of the guard tower a rifle began to fire. They angled the horses off to the side, along the slope, digging frantic heels into the flanks of the mustangs. And when was the mustang blood known to fail to respond to excitement? Every one of the three horses stretched out to full speed.

Two searchlights from the sides of the prison fingered the darkness, found the fugitives, and followed them. They slid in three beautifully clear silhouettes across the hillside.

Then a machine gun got to work. Its chatter ripped the night apart like the tearing of sailcloth. And the bullets kissed the air in closely grouped showers about the riders.

A half dozen bullets tore up the dust in front of Bray's horse. Another group hummed mournfully in his ears. The next burst would probably split the difference between the two ranges and blast the life out of his body.

But just then the horse dipped down into a gully. The

45

searchlight, for a moment, was cut off by a meager wall of shadow. Into that shadow the machine guns still poured their fire. But the three riders were now following the twists of the gully that led them up over the crest of the first hill. From the top they looked back. Two searchlights, as though inspired, at the same instant struck them. But they had remained long enough to see a column of horsemen rushing out from the main gate of the prison. Another squad of horse was spurring from the southern, another from the northern guardhouse.

Still the alarm bell kept up its roar. It no longer had such a brazen sound. It was more of a howling note, at that distance, that went wavering across the hills.

DILLON'S PLACE

DILLON'S PLACE STOOD HALF A MILE FROM THE EDGE of the town of Rusty Gulch, and fifty miles out of earshot of the clangor of the alarm bell of the Atwater prison. The three riders dropped the pursuit in the middle of the next day. They "borrowed" two changes of horses on the way, and finally left the armed hunters wandering through the mazes of a labyrinth of canyons north of Iron Mountain. Then they turned and drove with all their might for Rusty Gulch and Dillon's Place.

Because that was the home town of Jimmy Lovell, who had betrayed them; Jimmy Lovell, who had got away from the pursuit through the self-sacrifice of the other three on that day of days.

Jimmy Lovell would have all of their fortune now, and no doubt he was spending some of the half million amazing the people in his home town. For that was the style of Jimmy. That was the size of his heart and his

46

head. He was a fox, but he was a little fox. He would rather startle people by the spending of five-dollar bills than the squandering of thousands.

No, he would be back there at Rusty Gulch, as Phil Bray was sure, and in Rusty Gulch he would probably be at Dillon's Place. If only the three could reach that spot before the news of their break from prison could come to the ears of the guilty partner who had betrayed them!

So they rode hard and reached Dillon's Place outside of Rusty Gulch. It was night. The smell of the pines made the air seem honest and sweet. The stars were brighter than ever they had been, except when they were striving to show three fugitives on the roof of the Atwater prison. The three men dismounted among the trees near the road house and came slowly forward toward the light that burst out of the windows.

Dillon's Place was almost more famous for its lights than for its beer. There was a big gasoline lamp hanging in chains outside the front door to light up the watering troughs and all beneath the awning. There was another gasoline lamp of the same proportions hanging from the ceiling of the barroom. Men said that those lamps were dangerous affairs, that they might explode at any time, that if they exploded, every man within reach of the disturbance would be instantly killed by the terrible fumes, if not by the flames. Men complimented themselves on their brave willingness to endure such danger. They felt that Dillon himself was quite a hero.

Phil Bray, going ahead of his two companions, paused outside of the side window of the saloon with a strong shaft of the lamplight in his face.

He paused there and looked into the room with a strange expression of happiness in his eyes, as though he were drinking in a scene of surpassing beauty. He seemed to be listening to the sweetest music, also, though what he actually heard was a nasal tenor blatting out a cheap song in praise of whisky.

And what Phil Bray saw was a little red-headed man with a whimsical face capering on the top of a table with a whisky bottle in his hand, while a dozen other men leaned their elbows on the edge of the bar and laughed at the antics and the singing of the entertainer.

Phil Bray beckoned his two companions to approach. And at his shoulder they stood, agape, like him, with a sort of incredulous joy. For they recognized the singer as their former companion, the little traitor, Jimmy Lovell.

The three looked at one another speechlessly. They listened to the song. And they watched the flying feet of Jimmy Lovell. They had seen that dance before. Perhaps Jimmy would learn another sort of a dance step before long!

A sense of fate was on all three of them, for they felt that their delivery from the prison had been a continued miracle, and that they had been given their freedom so that they could work their just vengeance on rat-faced Jimmy Lovell.

A rider came to the front of the saloon at full gallop, halted his mustang with a jerk announced by the rattling of many pebbles, and came into the barroom. He was big, red-faced, red-necked. He came bustling in with the air of a person who has something important to announce, but he paused for a moment close to the doorway to grin at the capering picture of Jimmy Lovell.

As Jimmy ended his song and dance there was a great applause. Dillon, from behind the bar, was leaning his body to this side and to that, encouraging and inviting and multiplying the applause, closing his eyes and shaking his head, and laughing very heartily to indicate that he considered this fellow Lovell one of the most amusing chaps in the world.

"Stay up there, Jimmy!" cried Dillon. "You stay up there and sing us another, and then I'll set up two rounds for the whole house."

"Lemme kill him now!" breathed Joe Mantry. "Right now—to paste him in the mouth with a slug of lead. To turn that laugh of Jimmy's red. Come on, lemme finish him off."

"He's gotta see us. He's gotta know what's coming," said Phil Bray. "Hold your horses, Joe. Jimmy wouldn't know what hit him. And what would be the fun in that?"

Mantry did not argue, for the point was too patent.

Now the red-faced fellow who had just come in sauntered toward the bar, saying:

"Got some news, boys. I been down in Chester Lake, and the news, it just come in over the wire. There's been hell raised in the Atwater penitentiary! Three gents busted right loose!"

"Three!" cried the shrill, anxious voice of Jimmy Lovell. "What three? Three that was to hang yesterday morning—is that the three you mean?"

"Hey, how did you know that?" asked the newcomer.

"I guessed it!" shouted Jimmy Lovell. "The blockheads, they had those three in the death house. Couldn't they keep 'em there?"

"Why," said the red-faced man, "they got their hands on the warden through the bars of their cell, and they just about killed him, and they got the keys off of him. They jimmied up the lights and got down to the yard—"

Phil Bray said quietly: "Mantry, take the window.

49

This window here. Dave, take the back door. I'll take the front door. We'll let Jimmy see us, and then we'll paste him. I wanted to wait till we could get our hands on him—but after he gets this news, he's going to run like a jack rabbit and never stop running."

Bray left the window and hurried around the front of the building. Behind the wall he could hear the voice of the news bringer continuing:

"They get out to the gate and stick up the gatekeeper. They make him open up the gate, and they get through. By that time the warden was able to talk, and he gives the alarm. They start the bell ringing. The guard on top of the wall sees the three of them bolt from the gate, and starts shooting—"

Phil Bray stepped into the light of the doorway with a revolver in his hand.

On the table, Jimmy Lovell kept slowly prancing, lifting up his knees in an agony of anxiety as he heard the tidings.

"But they got guardhouses and searchlights upon the hills all around the Atwater pen," cried Lovell. "Nobody ever got out of the place. Nobody ever could. They got guardhouses and searchlights, and there's men and horses all ready at every one of the places. How could they get away?" He made an eloquently appealing gesture with the whisky bottle.

"They charged right at the first guardhouse. One of 'em shot the guard behind 'em off the wall. They smashed the light in the guardhouse and—"

This speech was cut short by a blood-chilling screech from the lips of Jimmy Lovell. His pointed face opened wide, and out of his throat the yell came swelling, louder and louder.

For in the lighted doorway he had seen Phil Bray and

50

the pointed revolver. He glanced to the side and saw Joe Mantry. He jerked his head over his shoulder and observed tall Dave Lister standing in the rear doorway.

He was cornered. He was tasting the perfect dread of death for half a second before it would strike him down. Then, whirling as if to leap, he hurled the bottle in his hand right into the gasoline lamp.

There was a booming explosion, with a harsh tinkling of glass in it. One wave of mingled light and shadow dashed through the room. Utter darkness followed with the yelling of frightened men and the groaning of the injured.

But there was no fire following the explosion. The violence of the outburst seemed to have extinguished all the flames. Or was it some strange accident that had kept the liberated gasoline from flaring up?

Phil Bray, knocked backward by surprise and the effect of the explosion, recovered himself and peered in vain into the turmoil of the dark, where figures were swaying here and there.

But he could make out nothing. He could not see one from another, only vague and fantastic shadows leaping. Two men rushed out the door and charged past him. One of them was small, very active, and dodged right and left like a snipe as he sprinted.

Jimmy Lovell?

Bray turned and went after him fast. The little figure darted around the corner of the building. Bray followed, saw the small form spring onto a horse on the farther side of the glimmering watering trough, and then the fugitive darted down the street.

It was Jimmy Lovell. There could be no doubt of that. It was Jimmy Lovell, riding for his life.

Bray stepped out into the street, leveled his Colt with

51

care, and emptied it. Three times he was sure that the bullets must have hit the mark. But the rider went on. Had Bray missed, after all?

He lowered the gun. Two men were charging toward him, demanding what he was up to.

"Taking a crack at the dirty swine that smashed that lamp," said Bray coolly, and, detaching himself from the others, he went back to the place where the horses had been left.

Mantry and Dave Lister were already there.

Lister was gibbering softly to himself, half out of his wits with rage and disappointment. Joe Mantry said nothing at all. They got into the saddle and rode back through the trees until they found an open trail. There they paused a moment, shoulder to shoulder.

"I done it," Bray said. "We should 'a' socked him full of lead as soon as we seen him. But I hoped that we could get our hands on him first and make him show us where he's hidden out the loot. Then I thought at least that we'd let him see what was coming to him before it arrived. I was all wrong all the way through."

"Drop it," said Mantry. "I would 'a' done the same. Where'll Jimmy go?"

"Into the deepest cover any gent ever found in the world," said Dave Lister. "I saw it in his eyes when he stood there on the table, screaming. I saw that he'd keep on running till he came to the end of the world."

"All right," said Bray. "We'll start for the end of the world. I don't want anything else out of life. I just want to get my hands on Jimmy Lovell."

LOVELL'S IDEA

LOVELL HAD BOLTED RIGHT ALONG THE OUT TRAIL away from Rusty Gulch. Bullets followed him. He rode for five minutes in a frenzy before he was able to look back and make sure that no one was pursuing him. Then he cut off from the trail, rounded back through open country, and came down into Rusty Gulch from the north.

The shack in which he was living sat back from the road a little distance. When he came up behind it he dismounted; then he crawled through the fence into the long grass of the back yard. The grass was wet with dew. The cold wetness soaked through his clothes, but the dew was not so cold as his heart.

The three of them must know where he lived. That was why they had not followed him up the road in their savage eagerness. They had simply turned back to his house, and there they were waiting for him.

But the house could be damned, for all of him. He only wanted to get to the well in the back yard.

He crawled on through the long grass. Dave Lister, he knew, had ears as keen as the ears of a fox. Dave would hear the slightest sound. Perhaps he had detected the rustling in the grass. So Jimmy Lovell went on an inch at a time, until he came out of the high grass into view of the well.

Bad luck again!

The Murphys, next door to him, were still sitting around the dining-room table. The window was open. He could see old Murphy sitting with the sleeves of his shirt turned up to the elbow, and the sleeves of the red flannel undershirt turned down to the wrist. Old Murphy believed that red flannel keeps away rheumatism.

But what was important was that a dim pallor of lamplight was shed through the open window, and stole across the very face of the well and its wooden cover.

Lying stretched out on the ground trembling, Lovell waited for a time. Three men and three guns might be, must be waiting for him in the black darkness of his house; but half a million dollars was inside that well!

He crawled on. Life was worth a lot, but what man's life was worth as much as half a million dollars?

He got into the field of the lamplight. Fear sickened him. As he crawled forward, his arms kept sagging and shuddering at the elbows. Then he reached the well.

He hoped that he could push up the edge of the wooden cover and reach down inside. But the cover was stuck in place. He had to rise to his knees in order to get greater lifting power. And when he rose, three guns might speak from the blackness of the empty door of his shack.

Suddenly he stood up. If voices hailed him, he would say that he was simply there to get a drink. Then he would run.

He gripped the edge of the wooden well cover, and lifted it, rolled it to the side. He dropped flat, reached down inside the well, and found the loose stone at the side, six inches above the level of the water. He pulled that stone out, laid it on the ground beside him, and reached into the cavity that appeared to his touch. The slickness of oiled silk rubbed against the tips of his fingers.

He pulled out the parcel with a sick feeling that it was about to drop from his fingers into the deep waters of the well. Then he dared not lift his head for fear he

54

should see three dark figures standing beside him.

One of them would laugh. That would be Joe Mantry. One of them would grab him by the back of the neck. That would be Phil Bray. He remembered the hands of Phil Bray, and how the fingers were square at the tips, and how the hair grew thick down to the first joints. It was a saying that no man in the world was stronger than Phil Bray in the hands.

Lovell raised the treasure to the ground level. He lifted his head—and there was no one near!

Suddenly a vast confidence came over him.

He got up, walked into his shack, into the dreadful, thick, warm darkness, lighted a lamp, and looked around him with a silent, sneering laugh.

No one else was there. He was in no danger. He felt as though it had been another man who had crawled with those trembling precautions through the cold of the grass like a snake.

That was what the three would call him in their thoughts—a snake! Well, snakes are hard to catch. They know how to go to earth. He would show them some more snaky tricks before he was through with them. And now what should he do?

Well, the mountains were deep and wild.

But the patience of Phil Bray would be more endless than the greatness of the wilderness.

He could flee to a seaport and take ship.

But Phil Bray would probably be waiting for him at the dock!

He could go and surrender the money and get the protection of the law. But how could the law protect him unless it closed him behind thick walls?

Besides, he knew that he would rather die than give up the money. Out there by the well he had suddenly known that with all the might of his soul. He would rather die. He would a lot rather die than give it up.

He sat down on the side of his bunk and took his face in his hands.

"I gotta think!" he whispered. "I gotta think of a smart thing."

For Bray was smart, and Bray knew all about him. Bray was the brains of the party, and always had been. Joe Mantry and Dave Lister were clever enough, but most of their wits were in their hands. Bray was the one to scheme and plan deeply, more deeply than other men. Above all, Bray knew Jimmy Lovell, despised him profoundly, but understood him.

Bray was the one who always used to say: "You fellows leave off jumping on Jimmy Lovell. Jimmy can do more than any of us—now and then."

Lovell grinned all over his rat face when he remembered that remark. In the finish he *had* showed them what he could do.

Bray, in spite of the protection he gave to Jimmy, was the one that Lovell had always specially hated, because Bray was the one who understood. Lovell, therefore, used to go to him now and then and say: "You're the one I buckle to, Phil. You're the one that I like. I don't like many people, but I like you. You'll see in the wind-up."

Yes, Bray had been able to see in the wind-up!

The other two, Mantry and Dave Lister, they would give up the hunt after a time. It was Bray who would never give it up and who would keep the others to the trail. There must be some shelter against Bray. But the law would not provide protection, and flight would not provide protection eventually.

It was a question of finding fire to fight fire.

Then a wild thought lifted Lovell slowly to his feet and made him stretch out his arms in welcome to it. For he had thought of a fire so great and strong that, compared with it, all the force of Phil Bray was no more than the flicker of an uncertain candle flame.

The rumor was strong in Rusty Gulch that, somewhere in the neighborhood of Iron Mountain, somewhere in the entangled forest, or above timber line among the lonely ravines, great Jim Silver was lurking in the solitudes. A wandering prospector was said to have seen him, and though Jim Silver fled at once from human eyes, the golden sheen of the stallion he rode had betrayed him still more. And the way that horse bounded up a slope and disappeared over the next ridge had proved that he must be Parade. The prospector had seen a gray form go through the brush on the trail of Jim Silver, and perhaps that was his tamed wolf, Frosty.

Suppose that Jimmy Lovell went to Silver and managed to find him? Suppose that Jimmy Lovell begged the great man's protection?

Well, Silver was the sort of a fool who found it hard to say "No." And once he extended the mantle of his protection over Lovell, what could even Bray and his two desperate companions accomplish to break through and get at their prey?

Lovell went to the cupboard in which he kept his food. He got a small sack of flour, part of a side of good bacon with plenty of streaks of the lean in it, some sugar, coffee, and a cooking kit. He put in salt and some hard-tack.

He got a Winchester and plenty of ammunition for it. How long he would be in the wilderness he could not tell. A month, two months, or as long as he could manage to cling to the side of the great Jim Silver.

Then he went out to his horse, mounted, and headed out of Rusty Gulch.

In the east the stars were growing dim. Presently the moon pushed up its triangle of fire, rose with a golden rim, rolled its wheel up the shaggy side of a mountain, and then detached itself from the earth and floated up into the open sky.

Silver was like that, thought the hunted man. He was detached from the world, and he moved above the concerns of ordinary mortals. And his light overwhelmed common men.

JIM SILVER

LOVELL TOOK THE STRAIGHTEST TRAILS FOR IRON Mountain. By noon, as he crossed the Camber Mountains, he was in sight of the big peak. The head of it was white, but below the snowcap it extended broad, dark shoulders that looked like metal and had given the peak its name. Still farther down, the forest commenced to clothe its sides, but the trees failed at a much lower level than they attained on neighboring mountains, as though the soil of Iron Mountain were hard for them to grapple with their roots.

It was noon when Lovell saw the peak. It was twilight, nevertheless, before he had managed to get to the valley at the base of it. A roar of water kept rushing through the great ravine. He climbed higher up the side of the mountain, through the dense woods, until he found a quieter place for his camp. He reached a little clearing in the woods, with a trickle of water, across the center of it and a patch of out-cropping rocks that would be ideal to shelter his fire from the wind.

There he unsaddled his mustang, built his fire, and cooked bacon and coffee, which he ate with hard-tack. There were plenty of pine needles, so he kicked together a quantity of them and laid his blankets over this soft bed. He sat down beside the embers of the fire and smoked cigarettes, brooding.

Fear had followed him all the way from Rusty Gulch, and fear would keep on companioning him. He looked anxiously toward the saddle. Half a million dollars was there. But where else could he leave it?

He was at this point in his thoughts when he felt eyes watching him. He felt them drilling into the small of his back, and, turning suddenly, he had a glimpse of something that faded back behind a bush.

He shrugged his shoulders. There were plenty of wild beasts in the woods, of course, but there were none that would attack a man—certainly not at this time of the year, when easier game was all about.

He had hardly a chance to slip into his reflections again, however, when he felt the eyes once more, and this time, looking sharply ahead of him, he saw the green gleaming of eyes among the shadows.

He snatched out a revolver, ready to fire. But the eyes had disappeared.

For a time a peculiar and unearthly fear troubled him, so that he could not move. Then he got up, lighted a match, and went to examine the place from which the eyes had been watching him.

There he found the footprints of a wolf, but prints of such a size that he could hardly convince himself that they were not made by a bear or a mountain lion.

No, they were the sign of a wolf, beyond any doubt! He measured the spread of the forepaws on his own hand, and went back to his dim little fire, shaking his head.

Then a thought stiffened him with a stroke of joy.

Huge prints of a wolf's foot? Why, it was the very thing that he had come to Iron Mountain to search for. Frosty's paws left on the ground a gigantic sign, because Frosty was a gigantic monster of his kind. It must be that strange companion of Jim Silver that had come to look in on the interloper. In that case, if he could follow the back trail of the wolf, might he not reach Jim Silver even sooner than he had dared to hope?

He went on into the brush, lighting matches, finding the sign of the wolf, losing it again. At last he felt that he had discovered the general line of the retreat of the big animal, and along that course he headed up the mountainside for a considerable distance, the big trees shifting slowly around him, the moon throwing patches of dazzling silver onto the ground here and there.

Then he came to a runlet of water, an incredible stream of brightness under the moon that seemed to drink up all of the rays and cast them confusedly out again. He paused to drink. His shadow stained the brilliant water with darkness. He picked up a handful of the water and drank. It was so cold that his fingers tingled; his palate ached a little from the iciness.

He stepped onto a small stone in the center of the stream. As he did so, a voice from behind him said:

"Hunting for something, stranger?"

The sudden unexpectedness of that speech plucked Jimmy Lovell around by the shoulder. He slipped off the rock he had been standing on and stood waist-deep in the tugging swiftness of the current, with a revolver ready for action.

But he saw nothing. The big trees stood in a dense row before him. Their black shadows lay evenly at their feet. The pine needles that covered the ground were moon-whitened, except where the shadows lay. And not a living thing was in sight!

Frightful suspicions darkened the mind of Jimmy Lovell. Out of books in his childhood he had read stories of werewolves. Fancies such as he did not dare to conceive haunted him in an instant. Then the same deep bass voice spoke to him from nowhere, saying:

"Put up that gun, please."

"Who are you?" asked Lovell.

"My name is Silver," said the other.

It was not pleasure that Lovell felt at first, but a shock of thrilling fear. During so many years he had dreaded that name—he and all his kind. During so many years he had heard the stories, the legends of this relentless pursuer of crime and criminals, this unpaid agent of the law, this protector of the defenseless. But now he felt that Jim Silver was his one resource. And he gasped:

"Thank Heaven! I was looking for you."

He put up his gun as he spoke. At the same time, from behind a tree there stepped out into the moonlight the biggest wolf that Jimmy Lovell had ever seen. The beast remained motionless, staring fearlessly at the stranger. After the wolf appeared a tall man with broad shoulders.

He did not seem so very big until he had walked close to Lovell. But his stature appeared to grow with every step that he made forward, until he was accepting the hand which Lovell held out to him. In the distance Jim Silver seemed rather made for speed and lightness of movement. It was only at close hand that one could appreciate the solid weight of those shoulders and the bulk and extent of the arms. He differed from other men as race horses differ from draft animals.

With, chilly awe, Lovell looked up at him.

"You're as big as they say," said Jimmy. "Did that wolf tell you that I was looking for you?"

"Frosty acted as though some one were on my trail," admitted Silver. "He can't tell *why* people want me, but he generally knows when they're on the trail."

"They say that he can talk to you," said Lovell, staring at the wolf, which waited on his master at a little distance.

Silver made a short gesture of denial, answering: "He's like any dog that's been well trained. That's all. He's not a bit cleverer than a thousand circus dogs. Most of the things that people say about him are bunk. Why do you want me? Are you bringing me news?"

"Aye," said Jimmy Lovell. "If you come back to my camp, I'll show you about the biggest news that you ever got in your life."

Silver made a pause. He seemed to be reading the man before him, line by line and feature by feature; it was not hard to guess that he did not altogether approve of what he saw.

"I'll go back with you," he said at last.

He whistled. Out of the distance a horse whinnied, not loudly. After a moment came a crackling of brush, and then there glided into the clearing the great stallion, Parade. He halted and tossed up his head as he saw the stranger. Then he sidled around behind his master.

Lovell looked on the horse almost with more awe than he had looked on the master, for he could remember the stories of how Parade had run down a fleeing man in spite of relayed horses that were used to save the fugitive; he could remember tales of how Parade had snatched Jim Silver time and again away from death.

62

There was no bit in the stallion's mouth. It was only a light cavalry saddle that was on his back. He looked almost as free and as wild as in the earlier days when he had roamed the desert as the lord of a herd. Creatures which are enslaved and subdued are dull of eye and low of head; but Parade had not ceased thinking for himself, even though he included his master in his thoughts.

The big horse followed the two men as Lovell showed the way back through the woods. On the way he kept turning in his mind various words, various ways of opening the conversation and making his proposals to Silver.

He was still in doubt when at last they came into the clearing where he had camped. Of his fire there remained one red eye alone. He took up some brush to freshen the fire to a blaze, and presently the warm, yellow light was flooding out in waves over the ground, and making thin filters of shadow dance among the pine trees. By that kinder light, Lovell looked at Silver again and wondered at the youth of the man.

The legend of him was so full and rich that it seemed. he must have spent a long lifetime in passing through so many adventures; but, as a matter of fact, he was not over thirty, perhaps. Yes, he might even be younger. He had taken off his broad-brimmed sombrero, and Lovell saw the two gray spots above the temples, looking like small, silver horns pushing through the rest of the hair. He had heard them mentioned a thousand times. It was by imitating those marks that Duff Gregor, in another day, had managed to complete his resemblance to the true Silver and make himself pass off as that famous and trusted man.

Famous, honest, trusted—and what was Jimmy Lovell to talk with him?

He thought of his stolen money. He would offer half of it if Silver guaranteed him safety.

No, because if the money were offered to Silver, that man would first of all inquire as to the source of it. And when he learned the truth, he would surely take it back to the ruined bank from which it had been stolen, far away in Elkdale. He would probably truss up Jimmy Lovell, also, and carry him along, to be received by the hands of the law.

What else could Lovell offer to tempt the man?

He stared helplessly at Jim Silver, and marked the faint smile that continued habitually on the lips of the big man. It was neither a sardonic nor an amused smile, but a mysterious expression of content, perhaps.

Suddenly Lovell exclaimed: "I was going to give you a good reason for wanting to see you. But there's no good trying to buy you, Jim Silver. I'll tell you plain and flat why I've come chasing to you—I'm afraid for my life!"

"Are you?" said the gentle voice of Silver.

"Three men are after me, and every one of 'em is full of guns and wants my hide."

"Why?"

"Three crooks. They broke out of jail a time back. I used to work with them, and they want me to work with 'em still. That's all. They want my scalp because I'm through with crooked business. They want my hide because I've made up my mind to go straight!"

He waited for the lie to take effect on the big man.

Silver said: "I've heard of things like that happening. Who are they?"

"Phil Bray, Dave Lister, the forger, Joe Mantry, the gunman. But Phil Bray is the dangerous one. He's the brains of the lot, and the best hand, too."

"Bray—Lister—Mantry," murmured Silver. "I don't think that I've seen them or heard of 'em before."

He sat down on a log. The wolf sat down at his feet and faced Lovell with eyes green with danger. If Lovell came a step too near, he was favored by a glimpse of long, needle-sharp fangs.

So Lovell kept back. He was glad, after all, to have an excuse for remaining at a little distance. He had an idea that Silver might otherwise detect the lies by watching the face of the man that conceived them.

In the background, Parade waited patiently, now and then turning his head to listen to a sound among the trees, now tossing up his mane as he sniffed at the wind that carried to him all manner of tidings beyond human perceptions.

"What do you want out of me?" asked Silver finally.

"My life!" exclaimed Jimmy Lovell.

Silver made a slow gesture, as though to indicate that life and death could not be in the range of his bestowal. At last he said: "I'm staying on Iron Mountain for about ten days. I'll be glad to have you with me for that time."

"Thanks!" breathed Jimmy Lovell. "And after that, will you let me tag along, Silver? You'll find I'm not a bad hand around a camp, and I can hunt meat for you. I'll keep you in fresh meat. I'll do the cooking and the cleaning up. I ain't proud. I'll take more than my half of the work, and when anything's wanted, I'll fetch and carry. If we get near a town, I'll buy what you want, and pay for it out of my own pocket. I won't be no burden to you. What about it?"

Silver ran his hand thoughtfully over the head of the wolf. The eyes of Frosty rolled back in acknowledgement of the caress. Then he ducked away from it, as though he feared that he might be blinded by the trailing fingers, and so prevented from maintaining his watch every instant upon the stranger.

Then Jim Silver said: "After about ten days, I'll have to start away. I don't know exactly where I'll have to go, but it will be away from Iron Mountain, and I'm afraid that I'll have to travel alone. I don't want to seem to turn you down. But I've got to admit that I'll have to travel by myself. If I can be of any use to you during the next ten days, I'm your man. After that I guess our trails will have to split up. I'm sorry."

There was no use appealing to him. The very gentleness of his voice was an assurance that he would not alter his mind in the least.

Jimmy Lovell nodded. Perhaps, during the ten days, by constantly watching his step, by entertaining with song and dance, by being useful on all occasions, he might, at the end of that period of probation, have attached himself to Jim Silver as the pilot fish is attached to the shark.

"Whatever you say goes for me," he said. "Ten days of life is better than ten days of lying dead, and that's where I'd be, except that I've run into you, Silver. And if I've got any luck, the three devils will tackle me while I'm with you—and after we've finished, maybe there won't be enough pieces of 'em left to put together and make one whole man."

FROSTY

FOR TEN DAYS THERE WAS NOTHING FOR JIMMY Lovell to fear, and he began to relax and enjoy himself in the presence of the strangest society that ever it had been his luck to know—a horse, a man, and a wolf, living together as a happy family.

That was all that Lovell could think of when he saw the three together. It was a family that had an intimate language of signs and sounds. It was a family bound together by the love of both animals for the man, and the love of the man for the pair of them. But there was a bitter animosity within that circle, also. There was never a time when the stallion ceased feeling fear and disgust for the wolf; there was never a time when the wolf ceased wishing to slit the throat of the great horse. So much was this true that Lovell said to Silver, on the second morning:

"How come that you ain't afraid to leave Frosty near that horse all the time?"

"They're not together all the time," answered Silver. "They have a rest from one another every now and then, and I watch them carefully. But if I were away for three days, I think that Frosty would murder Parade if he could catch him."

"Think of havin' a dog like Frosty around!" exclaimed Lovell enviously. "Better than a hired guard, I'd say he is. No hired guard would hunt around in the brush all day long and find out if trouble is walking your way."

"No," said Silver. "And he's useful in other ways. He has a book of things to do. You show him the page and he'll read it, all right."

Lovell gaped. It would not have surprised him a great deal to hear that the wolf actually was able to understand print. But now Silver, with a smile, pulled out a key ring that had on it a queer collection of ragged trifles. There was a bit of rabbit's foot, several pieces of metal, strips of leather, some bits of cloth, other odds and ends.

"That's the book of Frosty," said Silver. "He knows every page. Here's rabbits. If you want rabbit meat, Frosty will trot out and try to hunt for nothing else. If you want venison, here's a strip of the ear of a stag, and after Frosty scents that and gets the sign to start hunting, he'll go off and work all day, rounding through the country and trying to drive game to your gun."

"Hold on!" exclaimed Lovell incredulously.

Silver nodded. "He'll do that," he said. "It's hard for a wolf to catch a deer, but it's not so hard for a wolf to run it somewhere close to the direction that he wants to send it in. Here are other pages in his book. This leather off the pull straps of my boots. Here's my knife; here's my left-hand Colt, and here's the right-hand one. Here's my hat, my coat, my trousers. When he sniffs any of these things he knows that I want 'em."

Lovell had begun to frown. He tried to banish the frown from his face, but it kept on returning. He felt that his leg was being pulled more than a little.

Then he said: "Well, Silver, here's your knife right over here. It'd be quite a sight to me to see a wolf—or a dog—handle a knife."

Silver lifted a finger, and Frosty came to him. Under his nose, Silver displayed a single item of the odds and ends on the key ring, and Frosty immediately backed away with his nose in the air and his mane ruffling out.

It was plain that he detested everything connected with that knife.

He approached his master again.

"You're going to lose out on this," said Lovell, with a keen touch of pleasure in the thought that he might have found Silver out in an exaggeration. He could hear himself, later on, telling other men that Jim Silver could tell a lie, just like any other fellow in the world. He

68

would let people know that Jim Silver was not a whit better than ordinary mortality, and he would take a pleasure in letting them know it. "You're going to have your wolf miss—even if you point out where the knife is lying and tell your man to fetch it in!" He chuckled as he made this suggestion.

Silver eyed him calmly.

"I won't have to point to the knife," he said. "Frosty will find it."

Frosty was sniffing the knife sheath that was suspended from the belt of his master. Now, with a shake of his head, he backed away once more and pointed his nose into the wind, his eyes half closed.

Lovell fell silent. Half of his doubt fell away from him in an instant as he saw Frosty shift a bit across the wind and point into it again. But the wind blew from the lower part of the camp. It could not carry the scent of the knife to Frosty in his present position.

He shifted again, falling right back across the clearing to the farther side, close to the trees. He disappeared into the shrubbery.

"He's gone!" Lovell chuckled. "There's a trick that he misses, old son!"

Frosty, at that moment, reappeared, trotted straight up to the stump on which the knife was lying, and picked it up gingerly by the handle, his lips writhing away from the detested and terrible nearness of the sharp edge of the steel.

He carried that knife across to his master, laid it cautiously down at his feet, and then sprang back and shook out his mane with a strong shudder of his whole body. He did not need to speak words in order to express his strong detestation for work of this nature.

Lovell stood up and swore in admiration,

69

astonishment, and some regret.

"That's the damnedest thing I ever saw," he admitted. "What else has he got in that book of his?"

"Well, here's Parade," said Silver. "If he smells this bit of a leather rein, he'll go out and lead in Parade for me. That saves me a good many steps and a lot of time. I can let Parade range farther when I have Frosty to help me with him. I can let him range out of the distance of my whistle. He gets better grass a lot of the time that way. Want to see him bring in Parade?"

"No," said Lovell, scowling. "But you said that he'd run deer for you. I might mention that we ain't got any fresh meat on deck, and there's deer up there in the woods, or else I'm a liar. Did you say that he'd run in deer for you?"

"Not every time. Sometimes he can't find 'em, and sometimes they sprint away too fast for him and turn off to one side or the other, if they suspect that he's trying to drive them in a distinct direction. A wolf isn't very fast, you know. Frosty can't keep close to a stag that's under full way."

"Well," said Lovell, "I'd like to see what Frosty can do with the job. If he shows me *one* deer out of those woods—well, I'll eat my hat."

Silver regarded his companion for a moment out of narrowed eyes. Then he remarked:
"I don't want you to eat your hat. I'd rather see you eating venison. Come on, Frosty!"

He led the way with the wolf out of the camp to the edge of the woods, from which broad meadows extended toward a distant cloud of forest half a mile away. Now Silver showed Frosty and let him sniff at a strip of fur on the key ring, and waved him straight ahead.

Frosty made off in a line at a wolf's lope. On the edge

70

of the trees he paused to look back. Silver waved to him again, and the wolf disappeared straightway.

"We'll get down behind this brush and wait," said Silver, and dropped down to a comfortable position, with his rifle in hand. Lovell grinned dubiously and took up a position beside his companion, his own Winchester at the ready.

"Kind of hot here," said Lovell. "But maybe we'll only be half baked before we get tired of waiting for Frosty to turn up something out of those trees. There! Look there! He's out in that patch of clearing, running down the slope, not straight ahead through the trees. Now he's out of sight again!"

"He has to round in behind the wind, you see," suggested Silver.

"You mean that he's got brains enough to do that?" exclaimed Lovell almost angrily.

"You see," said Silver, "he hunted for himself for a long time, and he never came near starvation. I suppose there isn't much about deer hunting that he doesn't know. We'll wait a while and see!"

The minutes went on slowly. And after a time Lovell lifted his nasal but not unmusical voice in a song. It was barely ended before he heard Silver say:

"There you are!"

Looking across toward the opposite trees, he saw a fine stag dash out into the sunshine, slow up, and then bolt straight ahead as Frosty came bounding out in a hot pursuit.

Not straight toward the brush, but a little to the left of the two men the deer was fleeing.

"You take the shot," said Silver.

Lovell, widely agape, got to his knees. The nearest the deer would come, on its present line of flight, was

71

some hundred yards away from the brush. When it came to about that range, Lovell tried for it. But perhaps his excitement unsteadied his hand. At any rate, he missed. The deer, at the report of the rifle, merely lengthened its strides for the trees which were just ahead. As it reached them, Silver fired in turn, but the deer at once bounded out of view.

"Too bad!" said Lovell. "Too bad that we both missed him so clean. Maybe we had too much wolf in our eyes. Going to call in Frosty? Or will he come in off a blood trail as hot as that one?"

"He'd come in fast enough," said Silver. "But there's no need to call him. The deer is dead just inside the trees."

"Dead?" said Lovell. "It was running faster than ever, the last I seen."

"The last leap was the death leap," said Silver. "Come and see."

It was as he said. His bullet had clipped the stag right through the shoulder and the heart, and the deer lay dead, with lolling tongue and glassy eyes, just within the rim of the trees. Frosty sat panting at the head of the kill; he had not touched the fresh meat.

A new sort of awe came over Lovell.

"Silver," he said, "no wonder that folks are scared of you. If you can make horses think for you and wolves hunt and fetch and carry for you—"

"You'll see harder things done in any circus," answered Silver. "And I have a lot of spare time on my hands for the teaching."

"Then teach Frosty to like me, and to do what *I* tell him to do," suggested Lovell. "Every time I happen to come too close to him he acts as though he wanted to take my leg off!"

72

Silver shrugged his shoulders.

"I forgot to tell you one thing," he said. "Frosty learned to trust me against his will. I had the luck to find him down and out, and while he was getting his strength back, I managed to teach him that he could lean on me. Teach him the same thing, Lovell, and he'll be as good a friend to you as he ever was to me."

"Otherwise," said Lovell, "he's going to keep on looking at me like venison on the hoof?"

"Well," said Silver, "poor Frosty can only know a man by what he's seen him do."

There was enough in that speech to make Lovell suddenly stop talking and mind his business of cutting up the deer.

WAYLAND'S QUEST

HIGH UP ON IRON MOUNTAIN, HIGH ABOVE THE forests that dwindled to a low wall of green, high above the iron-colored rocks that extended beyond the timber line, high above the little lakes, in the region of perpetual snow, Oliver Wayland had traveled steadily on for several days, searching every recess, patient, enduring cold and hunger, doing without sleep by night and with very little food or rest by day.

He accepted all of this pain naturally and simply, because he felt assured that punishment of this sort must follow when a man has failed in his duty as he had failed on that day when three robbers with guns walked into the Elkdale bank. The thought that there was fate in the thing—above all, that he should hardly have finished hanging on the wall the picture of fearless Jim Silver before his own reign of terror began! Wayland kept the calm and smiling face of that man before him now. He knew that he could not be what Silver was, but he also knew that he could strive to lengthen his steps in the right direction. That was what he was doing now.

He descended, at last, not to actual timber line, but into the lower hollows, where the tough mountain shrubs were growing in specially favorite dells. There he had camped on this night, building a fire, putting at hand a sufficient quantity of fuel to refresh it, and then lying down.

He fell into a sound sleep. He was so exhausted that he could have slept on the back of a pitching mustang. But he wakened in the first gray of the morning, stiff with cold.

He got up, stamped to get the blood back into his feet, and then lay down to try to get another hour of sleep. But the bitterness of the cold, driven through him by the wind, refused to let him rest. He had to sit up, dizzy with weariness, and fairly hug the fire in order to get some of its heat into his shuddering body.

He was in that posture still when his burro—he was making his search for the robber on foot—jerked up its head from the scanty grass where it was browsing, and looked steadily toward its master and beyond him. At the same time a voice behind Wayland said:

"Take it easy, stranger. We want some of your chuck. We don't want anything else you've got. Stick up your hands!"

Wayland stuck them up. He wanted to laugh. He, the hunter after the bandit who had the loot of the Elkdale First National, was again held up, and sat like a fool with his arms above his head, at the mercy of more robbers.

He turned his head and saw three men standing in the

74

gray of the morning light. They had led their horses around the corner of the bluff that should have given shelter to Wayland and his fire. But the wind had seemed to blow all night right out of the heart of the sky. These three men, with the morning mist about them, and in the dull-gray light of the dawn, looked larger than human to Wayland. The tallest of the three advanced first, saying:

"You fool, why didn't you build two fires and sleep between 'em?"

Oliver Wayland said nothing. He merely gaped. It was the simplicity and the comfort of the idea that stung him to the bone.

"Is he heeled?" asked the deeper and heavier voice that came from the second of the trio.

The tall man came closer to Wayland, ran his hands over his clothes, and removed a Colt .45 that hung from his belt. He slept with that gun, as part of the necessity of getting used to it. He had never done much with weapons of any kind in his entire life. But he had had to bring along with him a weapon of some sort when he advanced along the trail of his present quarry. He had practiced with it every day, pointing it quickly, then leaning to see how closely it was aimed at the target. He blazed away a few rounds daily, also, and told himself that his marksmanship was constantly improving.

"Yeah. He's heeled," said the man who had fanned Wayland.

"Boys, it's Wayland! It's the cashier!" said the second man.

The mention of his own name peeled a veil from across the eyes of Wayland. He looked at the three and knew them, suddenly, to be Phil Bray, Joe Mantry, and Dave Lister, who had escaped from the prison on the

75

very night when he had gone there to try to persuade them to betray their own treacherous fourth companion, who had disappeared with the bank loot.

If he had picked over all the men of the world, he could hardly have chosen three more dangerous ones for encounter. They knew him, and he knew them. That was enough to make three men of their type murder him to insure his silence.

Something more than the cold of the wind ate into him.

"Yeah, it's Wayland, all right," said Lister, who had taken the gun. "Whatcha know, about that. Wayland!"

"He's out of luck," said Joe Mantry casually. "But where's his chuck?"

"Where's your chuck, Wayland?" asked Bray.

"There," said Wayland, nodding. "In that tarpaulin."

Mantry instantly uncovered it.

"A rind of bacon; some hard-tack; no coffee. Nothin' but tea. The food ain't fit for a dog!"

"I thought I'd better travel light," explained Wayland.

"Put down your hands," said Bray. "You're not dead yet—and we've got your gun. You're not dead yet."

"No, he's only dying," said Joe Mantry, taking a kick at the tarpaulin that he had thrown back over Wayland's provisions.

Wayland turned his pale, handsome face toward Mantry and said nothing. Joe Mantry, of all the three, had the convincing record as a man-killer.

"Why is he dying?" asked Bray.

"Look, chief," answered Dave Lister, the penman, "you wouldn't turn him loose, would you? After he's seen us up here? After he's spotted us? You wouldn't turn him loose to *ask* for trouble, would you?"

"Yeah. The whole regular army would be up here

76

after us in a coupla shakes," suggested Mantry. "What good is he, anyway?" he added bitterly. "There ain't any blood in him. And he eats dog food. Gosh, but my stomach's empty!"

"You kill him and you gotta kill a thousand," said Bray.

"We're not going to kill a thousand," argued Lister. "But look the facts in the eye. He knows us. He'll spread the news that we're up here."

"You kill him and you gotta kill a thousand," said Phil Bray.

"You ought to put an article in the paper," suggested Mantry sardonically. "You ought to send it in to the society editor somewhere. 'Up on Iron Mountain, enjoying a few weeks of rest, are Philip Bray, Joe Mantry, and Dave Lister, the murderers and bank robbers, recently of Atwater prison.' That's the sort of news you ought to publish. As good publish it as turn Wayland loose."

Wayland said nothing. Instead, he stared fixedly at the face of Bray, who seemed puzzled and kept shaking his head.

Suddenly Bray reached a decision.

"You can't go around murdering everybody you see that knows you," he declared. "You kill him and you've gotta kill a thousand," he reiterated for the third time. He waved his hand. "Get the idea out of your heads, boys," he concluded.

"This is the devil of an idea," argued Joe Mantry, lowering his head in a significant manner and glowering at his chief.

Dave Lister jabbed an elbow into Mantry.

"Quit it, Joe," he said. "Quit it, will you? The chief's always right. He's gotta be right."

"All right," agreed Mantry. "We'll say he's right again, but—"

He wound up by shrugging his shoulders.

Bray answered: "When you think I'm wrong, you can vote me down, the pair of you. There's certainly more than one way of crossing a mountain."

Joe Mantry, however, argued no more. He merely said: "Wayland, you ought to be dying, but Bray's brought you back to life."

Wayland felt it would be foolish to offer any thanks. In the meantime, the three set about cooking up the meager provisions of Wayland for a breakfast. They worked with remarkable speed and precision. No orders were given by Bray. Every man knew exactly where to turn his hand. And presently Wayland was being asked to sit down, at his own fire and partake of his own food.

He did so, still in a silence.

The three ate ravenously, rapidly. Then they lay back and smoked cigarettes. There had been practically no conversation for nearly an hour before Joe Mantry asked:

"What brings you up here, Longlegs?"

"I'm up here for my health," said Wayland calmly.

"You lie!" said Mantry, his fine, insolent eyes dwelling on Wayland with a leisurely contempt. "You lie. You're up here on a man trail and a treasure hunt."

Wayland said nothing.

Mantry turned to Bray.

"What about it, Phil?"

Phil Bray grinned and nodded. "Sure," he said. "The boy cashier, honest Oliver—he's up here trying to find the stolen money. Trying to find the man who has the loot. Going to give it back to the bank—going to open that bank up again, and get his job back, and

78

everything." He sat up suddenly. "You—Wayland!" he barked. "What makes you think that you'll find your man up here?"

"What makes you think that *you'll* find him here?" asked Wayland.

Bray stared. "You won't talk, eh?" he asked with dangerous calm.

"What's the use?" said Wayland. "If I really knew where the man was, I wouldn't be camping out here in the middle of the sky, would I?"

Dave Lister laughed suddenly. "That's a pretty good one," he remarked. "Out in the middle of the sky is about where he's camped, too! Hey, Wayland, you don't even know his name; and you never saw his face."

"No," admitted Wayland. "I never saw his face, and I don't know his name."

"What *do* you know?" asked Mantry angrily.

"I know the look of him when he's bent over a horse, riding fast," said Wayland. "That's all."

"Not a lot, is it?" demanded Bray.

"No. Not a lot. But better than nothing," answered Wayland.

"I kind of like this hombre," said Bray. "He means something when he says it." Then he added: "Look at here, Wayland. Open up and tell us why you picked on Iron Mountain for your hunt?"

"I've tried plenty of other places," answered Wayland. "But I've always thought, ever since the robbery, ever since that fourth man got away, that he must have known this part of the world pretty well. I thought that because of the way he was able to fade out of the picture. We were right on his heels, but he got clean away from us. Then I thought that he would probably keep in hiding for a while."

79

"Why? Why shouldn't he step right out for the East?"

"For fear somebody had recognized him during the chase," said Wayland. "I thought he'd lie low—for months, even, until all talk about the robbery was forgotten. And then he'd start on his long trip. Half a million dollars is worth a lot of care, I suppose. And if he were lying low in the mountains, he might pick Iron Mountain sooner than any other. Iron Mountain is cut to pieces with ravines. You could hide half a million men around here, let alone half a million dollars."

"He has brains," said Bray, nodding. "He's got brains, and he uses them. Just the same, you're wrong, partner. He didn't duck for cover—not right away. He took a chance on his face being known. But—well, we're up on Iron Mountain for the same reasons you are, take it all in all. That's a good reason for you to hit off on another trail, ain't it?"

Wayland waited, silent.

"I might even say," went on Bray, "that you have some reasons for starting off in a new direction—and keeping your mouth shut about seeing us up here."

"You think you could trust him that far?" Mantry sneered.

"I'm taking the chance," said Phil Bray.

Joe Mantry began: "Well, you're a—"

He left the word unsaid.

Wayland, rising, said:

"I'll get off Iron Mountain, and I'll keep my mouth shut. Besides, you can trust me, Bray. I know a white man when I see one."

He stood up.

Bray took Wayland's gun and gave it back.

"Can you use it?" he asked with a twisting grin.

"If I'm close up and have a lot of time," said

Wayland.

Bray laughed and slapped him on the shoulder.

"A bird like you," he said, "can always do a lot more than he thinks, or than other folks think. Now get out of here."

Wayland got out.

AN UNEXPECTED ENCOUNTER

WAYLAND WENT STRAIGHT DOWN THE SIDE OF IRON Mountain. In his heart there was a vast temptation to turn back and attempt to trace the three criminals in their pursuit of their treacherous fugitive, but Wayland had given his promise, and his word was sound as steel. So he went down the mountainside when the sun was rising and the forests were shut from view under a wavering sea of clouds all burning with the morning light.

The glory ended when he entered the fog. All about him the wet, black pine trees were dripping. The burro found a way more readily than the man, and Wayland followed the little animal rather blindly, as he often had followed it before, since he began his strange pilgrimage.

Presently the fog was above their heads. It changed into breaking clouds that blew apart. In the midmorning Wayland walked through a pleasant country of big groves, interspersed by green meadows, and the cheerful sound of running water was always in his ears. He wondered now at the years he had spent in the bank at Elkdale. He wondered at all men who live in cities, where space is rented by the cubic foot. Out here on the lower slopes of Iron Mountain, every living creature seemed to have a right to the ground it stepped on, and to some part of the blue sky overhead.

He looked upon himself and on his past life, and saw nothing but hollow failure. His boyhood ambition had been better—to get a patch of land and a few cows, and then watch the herd grow while he made pasture room for it, buying here and there in small parcels. That was a life that meant slow and patient work, but it meant days of free riding, also, and good air, and nights of sound sleeping. It meant filling the hands with something better than an accountant's pen.

He was thinking of these things, of the futility of all his life, of the emptiness, the hopelessness of this quest of his, when May Rucker rode a roan mustang toward him out of a thicket of pine trees. She came on him as suddenly as a thought. He let the burro go wandering on, bobbing its head a little with every step, and he did not recover his wits enough to drag off his hat before she had dismounted before him.

He could hardly realize that she was May Rucker, the banker's daughter. She was brown and rosy. It was hard for her to remain calm and sober, because smiling was sure to begin in a moment.

He had no idea how he should act, but she showed him. When he attempted to shake hands, she put up her face and made him kiss her. And she kept close to him, with her head bent back, smiling.

"You give up this silly business and come home with me," she said.

"What silly business?" asked he.

"Chasing a will-o'-the-wisp and half a million dollars. Let the money go hang. Father has paid every

82

penny to the depositors. And he still has the old ranch left, over and above. He's lost ten pounds, and learned how to swear at a mustang all over again. He says that squirrels are the only good bankers, because they can eat their own accounts. Now you come back home with me and go to work."

He stared at her, as though he were trying to swallow her words with his eyes.

"I can't go home with you," he said.

"Why not?"

"I've got to stay out here." He indicated the mountains with a vague gesture. "I can't go in. I've got to stay out here."

"You're going to lose your wits, like a sheep-herder," she said, shaking her head and frowning a little. "Wake up, Oliver."

"It shook up my wits a little, seeing you suddenly like this," said Wayland.

"How would it shake them up if you happened to whang into the thief you're hunting for?" she asked.

"I don't know," said honest Oliver Wayland. "I'm no great fighting man."

"Have you even got a gun?"

"Yes."

"Let's see it."

He pulled it out.

"Sink a bullet in that blazed pine over there," she commanded again.

He raised the gun, took careful aim, and fired. There was no result.

"I pulled a little to the right," said Wayland, shaking his head. "But now I'll allow for—"

She dragged the gun out of his hand. "Look!" she said, and fired carelessly, with hardly a glance at her target. But Wayland saw the bark fly.

"You can't shoot at all," she said to Wayland. "If you meet your man, he'll murder you—and that's that! Oliver, will you try to have some sense?"

"I'm trying to have it," he said, taking back the gun ruefully.

"Then give up this nonsense and come home with me, because you can see for yourself what would happen if you met your robber!"

He began to breathe hard. He squinted at the distance, not because he was trying to see anything there, but because he wanted to get the pretty face of the girl out of his eyes and out of his mind.

"Father wants you," she said. "He says the one bad thing he ever did in his life was blaming you for a thing you couldn't help—you and a wooden-legged man against three thugs! He's ashamed, and he wants you back. He says you'll make a better ranch foreman than you ever made a cashier. He says he wants to have you hear him swear at his pinto mustang. I can't stand listening, but perhaps you can. Oliver, come home with me this minute."

He smiled. The kindness, the bluffness, the real tenderness of old Rucker touched him. He was glad he a was looking at the distance, because he knew that there were tears in his eyes.

"How did you happen to come here?" he asked.

"Dad's ranch is only a few miles away. And I knew you were somewhere up in this direction. I've ridden up toward Iron Mountain every day for a week. Lew Ransome saw you down in Limber Gulch some time back. Today I had all the luck in a bunch. Here, grab that silly burro and we'll start back, Oliver."

He managed to swing his eyes around and look at her.

84

"I can't do it, May," said he.

"Can't do it? Why can't you do it?"

"I've told myself about the other job. I've got to try to finish it."

"Finish it? You might spend ten years."

"Yes, I might," said he.

All the smiling and the color were struck out of her face in an instant.

"Look at me, Oliver!" she pleaded.

"I'm looking at you," he said.

"No, you're staring right through me and past me. You're seeing the day when you came to our front a door and wanted to speak to me, and I came into the hall and wouldn't talk to you. I was afraid of dad. I went off to my room afterward. I cried. And then I beat the pillow to death and hated myself."

"I'm not thinking about that," said he.

"You are. And you're telling yourself that you'll find the robber and get back the money, and give it to dad, and tell him and me that you never want to see either of us again."

"I'm not thinking that," said Oliver Wayland huskily.

"But all that will happen," said she, her voice shrill, "is that you'll keep on the trail till you find your man, and then he'll shoot you deader than that dead tree over there. Oliver! Will you try to talk and make some sense? Look at me, Oliver!"

"I've got to stay on the job," said Wayland.

Afterward it seemed to him that he had been torn in two with pain. She had not talked a great deal more before she got on the roan and fled away on the horse swiftly, her head down.

She had begun to cry before she remounted. He told himself that he was a fool, that he always had been a fool, and that nothing could come of any attempt that he made in this life of his.

And then, striding forward, he began to follow the little burro down the slope, halting whenever the animal stopped to pluck at a good bit of grass.

They came to more woods, passed through them, and as they came toward the farther side, through a gap in the trees he saw a man riding a horse at full speed across the open ground beyond.

The rider was rushing away from him, crouched low over the pommel of the saddle, and into the dreaming, unhappy mind of Wayland came the thought that he had seen this picture before, of just such a rounded stoop of the shoulders as a man fled for his life.

Then he remembered. It was when he had stood before the bank in Elkdale and watched the four fugitives; it was when he had led the posse up the mountain trail and identified the three men who had entered the bank—and the fourth man who slunk so low when he tried to get `speed out of his horse.

And yonder—he knew it perfectly—was the man that he pursued!

HAND TO HAND

WAYLAND GOT OUT HIS REVOLVER. HE FOUND HIS fingers gripping it so hard that the whole gun shook in his grasp.

First he grabbed the burro and pulled it back a little farther inside the trees, for through them he could see that the stranger was amusing himself by putting his mustang through its paces, racing it back and forth, taking the air, and riding cruelly with whip and spur to get the most out of the gelding.

When Wayland saw the face of the man, he was sure that the stranger could not have been a member of the bank-robbing gang. He looked too much like a little rat; all the features ran out to a point. The eyes were set in close to the long nose. Those eyes glittered and shone uneasily. To be sure, the fellow looked like a beast of prey, but. he seemed too small, too weak, too sneaking to have associated with such a man as Phil Bray.

So Wayland held his hand and watched the other put the mustang through figure eights, and every time the man rode toward him, Wayland was sure that it was not the fellow he wanted, and every time the back of the man was turned, Wayland was confident that this was the fugitive he had followed before.

In the midst of the evolutions of the horse, a rabbit jumped up from a big tuft of grass and started kiting across the green open ground. At this, the stranger jerked his mustang to a halt so suddenly that it almost squatted on the ground, and, while it was still down, before it could rise, the man snatched out a revolver and fired.

The rabbit landed against the stump of a tree with a heavy thump and. fell back to the ground, dead, and blurred over with red.

The mind of Wayland changed again. He had thought the little man too inoffensive to be a bank robber; now he felt that the stranger was certainly too formidable with guns to be tackled by a novice like himself.

He watched his quarry dismount and pick up the rabbit in one hand. Wayland, in the meantime, slipped down the edge of the woods and came suddenly out behind the other. He was not five yards away as he said:

"Hands up!"

87

The bleeding rabbit dropped out of the hand of the stranger. His whole body wilted. He sagged at the knees. Then, by degrees, his head jerked around until he could look over his shoulder at Wayland.

"Up with them!" shouted Wayland, relief at his first step of success putting strength into his voice, strength into his body and his spirit. "I don't want to shoot you through the back, but—get those hands up!"

He came slowly closer as he spoke. He was not two strides away by this time, and now the hands of the stranger rose gradually, unevenly, to a level with his head.

At the same time he turned little by little, until he was facing Wayland.

"Who are you?" he asked.

"My name is Wayland. What's yours?"

The stranger blinked rapidly. Then he said: "Ralph Smith."

"What's your name?" repeated Wayland savagely.

The stranger was silent.

"It doesn't matter," said Wayland. "Tell me what you're doing out here."

"Seeing a friend of mine."

"What's his name?"

"Jim Silver."

"Great thunder!" exclaimed Wayland. "Jim Silver?"

Jimmy Lovell sneered at him. "That's his name," he agreed.

"Well," said Wayland, "maybe I'm wrong—maybe I'm all wrong, and I'll apologize afterward if I am. But in the meantime, I've got to search you!"

"You try to fan me," said Lovely "and you'll wish you hadn't."

"Maybe I shall," answered Wayland. "But I've got to

go through you and your saddle pack there."

He saw the nostrils of Lovell quiver and expand. The little black eyes shone brighter than ever.

"I'm going to fan you," said Wayland. "I'm sorry, but I've got to do it."

"What's your reason?" demanded Lovell. "Who you think I am?"

"I may have half a million reasons," said Wayland grimly. "Keep your hands up and turn your back to me again."

Lovell trembled like a leaf with his rage, but, seeming to realize that struggling was useless, he began to turn his body slowly. Wayland stepped closer. For one moment he was thinking about the future, not about his captive, and in that instant Lovell, still keeping his hands stretched high above his head, kicked straight for Wayland's gun.

He got it and the hand that held it. The blow tore the heavy Colt out of Wayland's grasp, battered his fingers to numbness, and Lovell dived at him, jerking at his own gun as he came in.

They struck together and went down, rolling. But Lovell was a cat. He had the cowardice of a cat and the fighting passion. He was much smaller than Wayland, but he knew how to handle himself. His gun stuck in its holster, so he snatched out a knife instead. He liked a knife better, when all was said and done, than any number of revolvers, when it came to hand-to-hand fighting.

Wayland, clumsily struggling, found his wind gone, and had a chance to curse the years in the bank that had softened his muscles and made him less than half a man.

Small as Lovell was, the little wild cat already was on top, and Wayland saw the flash of a knife.

That flash would have been enough to make most men yell for mercy. It merely made Wayland forget his weakness and fear. He set his jaw hard and gripped at the wrist of Lovell's knife hand. His lean fingers got hold and kept their grip. The face of Lovell, as he twisted and raged to tear the knife hand free, was an utterly detestable and hideous mask of murder. He frothed at the mouth in his vehement desire to drive the knife into this long, lanky fellow. Wayland chopped his fist against Lovell's temple.

Lovell stopped spitting and cursing like a mad cat. He stopped tugging to get at the knife. Wayland struck again and saw a far-away look in the eyes of the other.

A convulsive twist and heave of the body did the rest. Then he found himself sitting on top of the smaller man, with the knife safely in his own grip. He reached down and pulled the Colt from the holster, where it had stuck to resist Lovell's impatience.

Lovell had gone limp. He lay like a rag on the ground, staring at Wayland with a passive hate, while the fingers of Wayland probed the clothes, the pockets of his captive.

A wave of helpless rage came over Lovell.

"I had you down. I could have split your wishbone."

"You could," said Wayland. "You would have done it in another minute. But I'll give you a better break than that. If you haven't got what I want, I'll do you no harm."

He took a length of twine that he had found in the pocket of Lovell and tied the wrists of the man behind his back. Then he stood up. Lovell struggled to his feet and stood swaying, gasping, cursing under his breath.

"Jim Silver—what'll he do to you?" breathed Lovell. "What'll Jim do to you when he gets his big hands on you?"

"Nothing," said Wayland. "Not if I'm right and you're wrong."

He went to the mustang and opened the two saddle-bags. There was nothing of importance but odds and ends in one of them. The other was stuffed tight with paper, and that paper consisted of packets of green-backs.

Wayland untied the saddlebag and took it under his arm.

Then he turned back to Lovell. He could not hate the man as much as he wanted to.

"You're the fourth man, then," said Wayland.

"I deny everything," snarled Lovell. "I ain't going to talk. You lie—that's all you do. I found—the saddlebag. I found it—lying on the ground. I found it, and that's all."

"You're the fourth man," said Wayland calmly. "I ought to take you back to Elkdale and let the sheriff get you. It's my duty to do that. You're the sneak who cut adrift from your partners after they'd saved your life and put the loot in your hands. You deserve hanging a lot more than the rest of 'em, but I don't want any man to die on account of me. And I'm going to turn you loose. I know that I'm a fool, but I'm going to turn you loose."

The bandit batted his little bright eyes rapidly. He began to breathe more deeply, also.

"Listen to me, partner, will you?" he said.

"What's on your mind?" asked Wayland.

"If you get that loot—and you've got it—you can't use it—not while I'm adrift. But listen to me. We'll make a split. Fifty-fifty, and we both keep our mouths shut. I'll be your friend; I'll stand behind you and—"

91

Wayland lifted his hand.

"Not fifty-fifty," whined Lovell. "Two for you and one for me. That's fair, ain't it? I got hold of the stuff. I've kept it with three murdering devils on my trail. Listen to me, Wayland. Gimme a break, will you? There's more money there than any gent needs. There's—there's—half a million!"

Wayland waved his hand toward the distance.

"Get out!" he commanded.

Lovell pulled in a great breath, but the foul outburst of language that was choking him, he swallowed. He knew that life was more than he deserved to keep out of this adventure. So he managed to hold his tongue. He only glared at Wayland for another moment, and then jerked himself about and went up the slope.

He got to his mustang. Without the use of his hands, he could not mount the little horse or ride it, once in the saddle. So he took the reins and went on, leading the bronco behind him.

Wayland watched him go. He saw the man turn on the verge of the trees and look back at him with a con-vulsed face. He felt as a man feels when he has escaped from the toils of a monster of the sea. Lovell did not seem a mere human peril. There was a poisonous darkness about him that exceeded ordinary malice.

Wayland turned quickly away. He saw the spot where the grass had been trampled by his fight with Lovell. He saw the bloodstained body of the rabbit near by. A sudden fear came over him and dimmed the brightness of his happiness, for he realized that he had half a million dollars under his arm—and he was still a long distance from the vault of a safe bank!

A BIT OF PAPER

THE BEST WAY SEEMED THE STRAIGHTEST WAY. Oliver Wayland sighted the first two main landmarks on his course and headed for them. His way took him over the foot of Iron Mountain and finally through a long ravine that was as straight as the barrel of a rifle. The rocks came down in great jags on either side. The sun of the early afternoon filled the canyon with a mass of trembling flames, as it were. The brain was stunned, and the eye burned with the heat.

He accepted this pain gladly because he felt that it would be the final misery that he would have to endure. He was on the last road of his journey toward respectability, and therefore he lengthened his stride's along the way.

He had gone on for some time in this manner, regretting the need of whacking the burro before him until the little beast would shake its long ears and break into a trot that lasted never more than half a minute. He had tied to the badly built pack the saddlebag which contained the treasure. It bumped and thumped along the side of the burro as the burden bearer humped to escape the blows of the man. But finally the burro would break again into the trot and go impatiently forward, shaking its head, its tiny, polished hoofs twinkling rapidly. If Wayland looked down at its feet, it always seemed to be going briskly, but the steps were very small.

He wondered how many tens of thousands of men had steered their courses through this wilderness, sighting the landmarks through the long ears of burros.

93

He was still wondering this when it occurred to him that the state of the treasure needed some examination. Suppose, for instance, that the robber had removed a portion of it—might not Rucker blame the loss on Wayland?

So Wayland walked up beside the burro, pulled the mouth of the saddlebag ajar, and looked inside it. He saw, within, the jumbled mass of the money, the little packages wedged together without any order, and some of the brown paper bands that secured the parcels had broken and lay loosely on top of the load. He smiled when he saw his own handwriting on one: "250, 5s." Fifty five-dollar bills in the bundle that wrapper had once surrounded.

Fifty fives. A good, tidy wad of money all in itself. How many months would a cow-puncher have to work in order to save that much clear? It suddenly seemed wonderful to Wayland that all the men of the world were not bandits. After all, is not our ordinary routine of living like that of a prison? Does not the demand of our labors make us retire early and rise early? Are we not subject to taskmasters? Do we not feel the whip if we do wrong?

All slaves, all prisoners, it seemed to Wayland, were the men of this world, of whom he was one. And was it not better to take the great chance in order to win a fortune at a stroke?

He had never thought about money except as a tool in the hands of an ambitious, industrious man. But in the burning heat of this valley he thought of it as leisure, infinite, lifelong leisure. A man with plenty of money could sit at ease and watch the world go by. He could visit far lands. He could follow the sun and make winter into summer. He could be as free as a bird from toil and trouble. Above all, he could command his own destinies, and no other human could bid him come or go!

Suppose, then, that he should change his course, and go, not to Elkdale to make a return of the hard cash, but to the nearest railroad station to board a train for liberty?

He had been honest all the days of his life, but now temptation made his eyes shine and his heart jump. Afterward he remembered May Rucker and the ranch to which he had been invited. Within us there is a voice that must be obeyed. And he resolutely shook his head and fastened his mind on duty and the right.

Absently he picked from the top of the saddlebag the loose brown wrapper that had "$250" written on the top of it in his own hand.

He shoved the crinkling paper into his coat pocket and walked on, pulling up the mouth of the saddlebag again. The burro, as he fell behind, once more took a straight road up the bottom of the hot ravine.

Sweat was running off the beast, showing in little black streaks through the tough, mouse-colored hair. Sweat was running on the forehead and cheek of Wayland. The sun scorched his shoulders; it hammered on his back. In more than one way, he felt that he was going through a trial by fire.

Then, turning a sharp corner of the ravine, he was gladdened by the sound of running water. It made the burro quicken its steps, almost to a run. Furthermore, there was something for Wayland to see other than the little stream that worked its way with faint murmurs into a big pool. The additional scenery was a group of three men, and his heart sank as he recognized Bray, Lister, and Mantry.

Bray and Lister hardly mattered so much, but that

95

beautiful, sleek wild cat, Joe Mantry—he was the danger spot in the picture.

It was Mantry who spotted him now and sang out:

"Well, upon my word, here's honest Oliver, the cashier! What is he still doing on Iron Mountain?"

The three had been sitting on rocks near the pool, watching their horses drink: They stood up now, and looked gloomily at Wayland. For his own part, he waved at them and tried to be cheerful. It was far too late to try to retreat. The burro was already sticking its muzzle into the pool and switching its ridiculous tail with content as it started the water gurgling down its throat.

"Hello, boys," said Wayland. "Didn't expect to see you again today."

Phil Bray began to make a cigarette, staring down at his work. Wayland took that for a bad sign. It was Dave Lister who said:

"We told you to get off Iron Mountain. You're still here. What does that mean?"

"I'm off it—just about," said Wayland pleasantly. "I made up my mind that I'd been a fool long enough. I was starting home."

"What's home to you?" snapped Mantry.

"Elkdale, of course," answered Wayland.

"How come Elkdale?" asked Lister. "You ain't welcome in that town, I'd say. Not more'n a snake. The Elkdale folks know that you stood by while their bank was robbed. Fellows like that would be apt to call you a yellow dog, Wayland. So how does it come that Elkdale is still your home town?"

"When you've been long enough in a place," said Wayland, "it doesn't matter much how people treat you. You always expect to get back on the top level again."

96

"From newsboy to president," remarked Mantry, sneering. "Patient, honest, humble—that's what you are, Wayland."

Oliver Wayland took no heed of the deliberate insults. He had something more than his own dignity in his thoughts and in his charge at this moment.

"You're not heading back for Elkdale. You ain't given up your job," insisted Dave Lister.

"That's what I've done, though. I'm not hunting for the stolen cash any more," said Wayland.

"Then you've got it with you, is why," announced Lister.

The guess shocked Wayland to the heart.

"Aw, shut up and quit joking, Dave," said Mantry. "If he bumped into that hombre he'd get his heart ripped out of him."

"These simple birds do a lot of funny things sometimes," commented Dave Lister. "But how come that you didn't get off the mountain when we told you to get, Wayland? That's what we gotta talk about, I guess."

"I'm about off of it," repeated Wayland. "Then I decided to quit the hunt, and I took a bee line for Elkdale."

"Where does Elkdale lie, Dave?" asked Mantry.

"Straight ahead," said Lister. "He might be telling the truth. I dunno what else there is for him to tell. Listen, Phil, do we let him go through us again?"

Phil Bray jerked up his head and breathed out a cloud of smoke slowly.

"I don't care," he said. "I don't care what you do with him."

He turned his back and began to tighten the cinch of his horse, which he had loosened. Mantry and Lister exchanged glances.

"Aw, what's the use?" said Lister finally.

"Yeah, what's the use?" agreed Mantry. "I'd sort of like to take a fall out of this big hunk. But what's the use. Let him run?"

"Yeah, let him run."

Mantry jerked a thumb over his shoulder.

"Get out!" he commanded.

Wayland nodded. "Thanks," he said. "This is white of you fellows. You can depend on me not to blow any news about you."

He walked on, pulling a bandanna from his coat pocket to wipe his face. And as he did so, a little piece of paper came out with the silk and dropped with a rustle to the ground.

He knew what it was—the bit of brown paper that he had placed in his pocket. from the saddlebag, with the sum of money neatly inscribed on the top of it. He was minded to stoop and pick it up. On second thought he decided that this would attract too much attention to it. The wind, after all, would soon roll it out of the way.

So he walked on, with a chill tingling passing up his spine. His heels lightened and rose from the ground of his own will. He walked as though he were expecting a bullet at any moment through the middle of his body.

But not until he was rounding the next corner of the ravine, at a little distance, did he venture a glance back, and then he saw Phil Bray leaning to pick up from the ground the paper which he had dropped!

He could not, of course, stop to discover what the three would make of that wisp of paper, or whether they would at once recognize the thing as the wrapping which had once been around a good, thick wad of greenbacks. But he could take it for granted that their

98

wits would be a little sharper than those of ordinary men.

He was out of sight now.

He had to flee. They would doubtless be after him soon. And they had horses, while he was on foot with only a burro, which any man could outrun!

To his right, the wall of the ravine consisted of a great rubble of broken stone, gravel, small rocks, big ones, boulders as big as a house. It was a sort of giant's staircase, but it would have to serve him now. He snatched the saddlebag from the side of the burro, turned, and bolted up among the rocks as fast as he could run.

After him, thin and small, wavered the voice of Lister, loudly shouting: "Wayland! Hey, come back here!"

He ran on, his heart thundering so fast that already he was weak with fear. He looked down after a moment and saw three riders sweep around the elbow turn of the canyon. He dived for shelter behind a great rock, but their wild yell of excitement told him that they had spotted him with the first glance.

THE PURSUIT

HE WENT ON, FULL SPEED. A MOMENT LATER HE HAD A chance to look down, and saw all three of them after him, eager as hunting dogs. Lister might look too long and weak in the legs, but, in fact, he had the agility of a leaping deer. Mantry looked an athlete, and climbed like one. And as for Phil Bray, he was the sort of man that one could have told at a glance as one of the toughest and the strongest to be found.

99

They came swarming up over the rocks, and Wayland knew, at once, that he had only one way to escape—by using his wits.

The top of the ravine wall was not so very far above him, but he made no further effort to reach it. Instead, he pulled off his boots, dropped them in a crevice between two boulders, and turned sharply to the right, crawling among the rocks.

He heard the panting of the men as they climbed. He heard the gritting of their boots on the stones, the clank of steel, at least once—and then they were gone above him, toward the top of the ridge.

He was at once under way down the slope, moving rapidly, silently. He had to take chances now, because those fellows were foxes, and they might read his mind when they discovered that he was not at the top of the ridge or visible on the farther side of it.

So Oliver Wayland exposed himself recklessly all the way to the bottom of the slope, only taking special heed that no stone should be dislodged and rolled noisily down before him.

He gained the bottom, and looked up for the first time. He saw Joe Mantry standing slender and alert on the top of the slope, a rifle flashing in his hands. But Joe Mantry had his back turned, and was looking the opposite way.

Just at hand were the three horses. Should he try to take them all with him, or only select the fastest-looking of the lot and bolt on that one?'

He decided on the second expedient. After all, he must trust to speed in the get-away rather than the chance of being followed, for riflemen like those desperadoes were not apt to miss, and their gunfire from the ridge would command the valley for a distance up and down it.

He picked on the horse of Phil Bray. It was not tall, but it was built long and low, with good, square quarters, and a rangy neck that promised striding ability. So he pitched himself into the saddle and walked the horse around the bend.

Not a shout, not a bullet, had followed him so far!

He let the horse break into a soft jog. Presently, looking back again, he saw Joe Mantry still on the ridge, for, as the distance increased, the angling bend of the canyon was no longer a protection, and Mantry, on his high post, stood over the whole ravine like a hawk on hovering wing.

It seemed as though Wayland's glance had pulled the eye of Mantry toward him. At that instant the sentinel turned, saw his man, and pitched the butt of his rifle against his shoulder.

Wayland, dropping forward in the saddle with a groan, shot the mustang away at full speed.

A humming sound twitched through the air over his head; something thudded against a rock not far away before him.

That was a bullet, he knew. He lay down flatter on the back of the gelding, and the mustang responded by sprinting with all its might. Just ahead there was an S-turn which would shut away even the high post of Mantry from any view of him.

That was the goal of Wayland.

Then something thudded on the side of the saddle, and the horse staggered under him. The hind legs of the mustang seemed to be dragging in deep mud, while its forelegs still struggled to keep going at full gallop.

The gelding began to sag and stagger all to one side.

Wayland understood then. He grabbed the saddlebag

that held the treasure, tucked it under his arm, and slid down to the ground just as a second bullet thudded through the skull of the horse and dropped it dead.

Glancing back, he could see Mantry lying out on the rock, taking good aim. Big Phil Bray and Lister were already legging it down the slope, leaping like mountain goats, regardless of brittle bones.

Wayland, as he started to run, dodged this way and that. Bullets sang past him. He was sure that he was lost, but he kept on struggling.

A slug struck fire out of a granite boulder beside him. Another twitched at the hair of his head. And then he had dodged out of fire range around the corner and into the windings of the S-turn.

Beyond that complicated turn there was a branching of tributary ravines, one to the right and one to the left. If ever he could manage to keep his wind until he reached the triple forking of the ways, he would take the right-hand turn and trust to fortune that the enemy would either go straight ahead or sweep to the left.

Behind him now he heard the rattling of the hoofs of horses raising out of the canyon, as from between two sounding boards, reduplicated echoes in a long roar.

That noise seemed sometimes near, and sometimes it appeared to recede. Now Wayland's lungs were on fire. His knees were numb. He beat them down with his hands to give himself greater speed, but he was at a stagger when he came to the end of the S-turn and saw the ravines forking way out to either side.

He followed his original intention by swerving to the right, for the mouth of the ravine was narrow, and the pitch of the shadow right across it gave him promise of many windings. Perhaps it would immediately climb to the uplands, and there, among the trees, he would have ten-fold greater chance of getting away.

Or suppose that he were to drop from his hand the cursed weight of the saddlebag that anchored him and kept his feet dragging? He was running for his life now, but if he gave up the prize, he would be as safe from those three thugs as though he were walking among friends down the main street of Elkdale.

Perhaps it was that thought of the sunny, dusty main street of Elkdale that decided him. For if he returned without the object of his quest, he would have few friends or none to walk beside him. He would remain, to the end of his days, a suspected man; worst of all, he would be suspect to himself.

That was why he ran straight ahead, but presently the last of his breath came groaning from his lips, for the ravine that had commenced in such a narrow gorge now opened up suddenly into a considerable valley floor, with a heap of rock like the beginning, or the wreckage, of a small hill in the middle of it.

He slowed to a dogtrot, despairing, and on top of that despair he heard the crashing of iron-shod hoofs on the rocks at the entrance of the gorge.

The world spun around him and over him. He seemed to be running with the blue of the sky under his feet. There was only one way for him to head, and that was straight at the heap of great rocks in the middle of the valley, and that was, accordingly, his goal.

He reached it with bullets all around him. Over his shoulder he saw that they had entered his own part of the canyon, and were fanning out, firing as they galloped. Behind the first rock he sank down and waited for death.

SILVER'S DECISION

LOVELL WENT BACK TOWARD THE CAMP OF JIM SILVER, whining all the way—whining and snarling. Sometimes the passion of his shame, hate, and rage so overcame him that he had to pause. His body stiffened. He writhed in stiff little convulsions before he could walk on again. He cursed the slippery pine needles under his feet, the horse that pulled back on the reins against his tied hands, the blue of the sky over him he cursed, because it had seen him humbled this day.

When he got to the camp, Silver was not there; neither was Parade.

But the quarters of a deer hung from a low branch of a pine tree, where Silver must have placed the meat not long before, and under the dripping venison lay Frosty. He gave no sign of seeing the man approach, but kept his big head down on his paws. He lay as still as a bullet could ever have laid him, with the wind ruffling in the gray of his mane now and then. There was only one point of life, and that was the eye, half shut, but open enough to reveal a glimmering green. But he used them not even with a side glance to mark Lovell.

Jimmy Lovell paused, released his mustang, and cursed the wolf. Not that he wanted any of the venison, but because he knew perfectly well that Frosty lay still in the hope that Lovell would try to get at that meat and give the wolf a chance to sink his teeth in the man. Silver's control over the beast was not sufficient to make it like Lovell or accept the new man in the camp. Frosty would endure the stranger, and that was all. If they encountered face to face in moving about the camp, the wolf halted and would not give way an inch. So

104

Lovell hated the big brute with all his heart, for Frosty, was to the bandit a continual reminder of the superiority of Silver.

When he had finished cursing the wolf, he turned his attention to Silver, and cursed him in turn for being away from the camp. Silver had promised him ten days of protection on Iron Mountain; at least, Silver had permitted him to stay at the camp during that interval, and it would go hard, Lovell felt, if he could not induce that famous man to take the trail of Wayland and recover the lost treasure.

But there was no sign of Silver for a long time. For hours, Lovell had nothing to do but roam around the camp, groaning, trying to chafe through the rope that confined his wrists, and it was late in the afternoon before Silver appeared.

As usual, there was no sign of his approach. At one moment there was not a trace of him near the camp, except that Frosty sat up suddenly and yawned his red mouth open, and showed Lovell the pearly whiteness of his teeth. And a moment after that Silver was standing inside the circle of the trees, with Parade a little behind.

The silence of those comings and goings of Silver always annoyed Lovell. He knew that there were no idle tricks in Silver, and that the man acted merely as nature bade him; his secrecy of movement was a necessity, when there were so many rascals in the world eager to put a knife between his ribs, or a bullet through his brain. Nevertheless, Lovell hated all his ways, and his quiet stealth above all things. He could not look at Silver without feeling that the big man was an example of human nature as God intended it to be. In the gentle and fearless face of Silver he was able to see his own wretched meanness of soul. The more obligations were piled upon him, the more he detested his benefactor.

When at last Silver came into the camp with his noiseless step, and Parade like a great, brilliant, drifting ghost behind him, Lovell was sitting on a fallen log, his hands still bound behind his back, and his head bowed. He gave Silver no greeting, and waited for an exclamation, for an expression of concern. His heart swelled with rage when Silver spoke not a word, but, stepping behind him, drew a knife and cut the rope that had held Lovell helpless.

Silver slipped the hunting knife back into its sheath, leaned against a tree, and made a cigarette.

That was all. He permitted no questions to escape his lips.

Frosty glided to him, looked up into his face, and then disappeared among the trees.

The anger and grief in the heart of Lovell swelled higher than ever. There seemed to be a silent language by which the man and the wolf communicated with one another, shutting him out, making him a futile eavesdropper in that camp. No doubt Frosty had asked permission to go off hunting on his own, and his master, with some imperceptible gesture, had let him go.

"Well," said Lovell, "you don't care. I might 'a' known you wouldn't!"

Silver said nothing at all. His calm eyes considered Lovell without favor or distaste. There seemed to be no passion in Silver. He was like a rock that could not be budged. At least, Lovell never had been able to move him—and yet he knew that this was the man who had raged like a storm on the trail of Barry Christian and other great criminals.

Silver took off his hat and dropped it on top of a small shrub. He put back his head and let the wind go ruffling through his hair. The content of the wilderness and the free life was in his eyes.

"I'm the fool of the world!" groaned Lovell suddenly. "Here I been trusting everything to you—and I've been robbed! Robbed right here under the nose of the great Jim Silver! I've been hawked at right under the nose of the eagle, and he sits on his perch and blinks and doesn't care!"

"I'm sorry," said Silver calmly.

"No," declared Lovell, "you ain't sorry. If you were sorry, you'd do something about it. If I was Taxi, or one of your other friends, you'd be raging along on the trail of the thug that grabbed me. You'd be right after him this minute. But you don't care. What's a promise to you?"

"Promise?" said Silver, startled.

"Aye, you promised that you'd keep me safe for ten days on Iron Mountain."

"I don't remember that."

"Sure you don't. Nobody remembers what they want to forget!"

"I told you that you were welcome to stay with me as long as I was on Iron Mountain. That was all."

"*You* think that was all, but I remember different," lied Lovell. "You told me that I'd be safe here with you. That's what you said. For ten days I wouldn't have to worry. Well, that's the way it turns out, too. Before the ten days are over, I'm not worrying. No! Because I've got nothing left to worry about."

"Did I promise that I'd take care of you?" asked Silver.

"Did you? Of course you did! Why else would I 'a' been hanging around here? To admire the wolf, maybe, or listen to the silence?"

107

He saw the mouth of Silver pinch a little in profound distaste. But Lovell did not care. He wanted to spur the big man into action, and he did not care how deep he roweled the hero, if only he could start him moving.

"A saddlebag was taken away from you," said Silver finally.

"Hey! Did you see the whole thing?" exclaimed Lovell.

"No," said Silver. "I see the saddlebag is missing. That's all."

"You see everything," said Lovell gloomily, "even when I think that you're seeing nothing."

That unwilling compliment Silver passed over in silence. But he said afterward: "What was in the saddlebag?"

"That don't make any difference," said Lovell. "There was things in it that I couldn't afford to lose— and it was stolen right here on your own mountain, right here under your nose!"

"Was there money in that bag?" asked Silver calmly.

"No matter what there was—it was mine!" exclaimed Jimmy Lovell. "What difference does it make what there was in that bag?"

"It makes a little difference," said Silver. "I need to know. Was there money in the bag?"

"Yeah, and what if there was?" asked Lovell, goose flesh prickling on his body as he felt himself approaching dangerous ground.

"Stolen money?" went on Silver.

"Damn!" cried Lovell. "You ain't going to help me. You don't want to help. You only want to ask questions!"

"I'm going to help you," said Silver. "That is, I'll help except in one case. But I want to know a little of the truth first. Was it stolen money?"

"I've been robbed!" cried Lovell woefully, "and you sit around and ask questions, is all you do!"

"You're a thief yourself, Lovell," said Jim Silver.

"Me?" shouted Lovell, and then he was silent, staring. At last he burst out: "What makes you think that—"

"Everything about you," said Jim Silver. "Your ways with your hands and your eyes. And besides, people who hate the world always have done harm in it. You hate the world, Lovell. I've never heard good words from you for any one. You're as bitter as poison about every one."

"I got my reasons," said Lovell gloomily.

"I'm asking you again, was there stolen money in that bag?"

"Yes," said Lovell suddenly. He made a gesture of surrender. "You wanta know—and there you have it. The money was stole! But," he went on, shouting out the words in a fury, "it was taken away from me while I was with you—after you'd promised to watch out for me. I ask you, is that what a man has got a right to expect from Jim Silver?"

Silver raised his hand, and the other was silent.

"Who was the man that took the stuff away from you? Did he own it?"

"No," cried Lovell. "He didn't have no more right to it than—"

"Than you have?"

"I went through hell to get it! I'm in hell now!" groaned Lovell. "And all you do is ask questions."

"One man got at you. What sort of a man?"

"How d'you know it was only one man?" demanded Lovell, curiosity getting the better of him for an instant.

"You wouldn't resist more than one man," answered

Silver calmly. "And today you *did* resist."

"I wish I'd split his wishbone for him," snarled Lovell. "I had the chance, too, and my gun stuck in the holster."

"You ought to file the sights off your gun," suggested Silver, smiling a little.

"I can't file a gun. I can't shoot by instinct," said Lovell. "You know that. I ain't like you! And my gun stuck. Even then, I got right in at him."

"He had a hard set of knuckles, eh?" suggested Silver.

"You know him? You met him?" asked Lovell. "You just been stringing me along all this while?"

"No," answered Silver. "But I can see the knuckle marks on your temple."

Lovell writhed his lips, but said nothing.

"You've come up here with stolen money. Another thief took the loot away from you. You think I ought to get it back for you," said Silver, slowly summarizing the case. "And, as a matter of fact, I don't know *what* I ought to do."

He fell into a moment of musing, and a thousand words rushed up in the throat of Lovell. For the first time he had real hope that he might be able to persuade the big man to help him. The trail, as far as Lovell was concerned, was lost long before; but Silver, with his uncanny eyes and sense of things, helped by the hair-trigger sense of smell with which Frosty was armed, might unravel even older and harder trail problems than this one.

And then inspiration descended upon Lovell. He was choking with desire to appeal, but he gripped his teeth hard together and spoke not a word. He could see that something in the mind of Silver was working, however obscurely, on his behalf, and he was inspired to let that inward spirit react upon Silver instead of trying to push his own case.

Jim Silver began to stride up and down.

Then, pausing at the edge of the camp, he tipped back his head and sent a long whistle screeching through the woods. The sound was not great in volume to one close at hand, but along his nerves Lovell could feel the knife-like penetrating of the vibrations. The whistle ended, and the thin echoes presently were still.

Silver had called in the wolf, and that could only mean one thing.

Lovell stood up, stiff and trembling with hope and with fear.

Silver said to him: "This is the rottenest business that I've ever been mixed up in. I don't know that I'm doing right. But if I promised to take care of you while you were with me on Iron Mountain—mind you, don't remember having made that promise—then I've got to keep my word. I'm going to trace down that money and give it back to you, and then I hope you'll get out of my sight and never make me rest eyes on you again."

DEATH IN THE AIR

WHEN WAYLAND HAD GAINED THE SHELTER OF THE rocks, he waited for a few moments, convinced that the riders would presently be at him. Phil Bray was off to the left, riding one horse. The other animal had to carry both Mantry and tall Dave Lister, but it had seemed able to keep up with the mustang which had but a single burden. And those three savage men would surely be at Wayland in another moment.

A full minute passed, while Wayland lay gasping,

before he realized that he was being given the grace of a little intermission from danger. He ventured to look up above the rocks that were sheltering him, and he saw one horse in full view, another out of sight on the other side of the hill of rocks, perhaps. But of the three men he could see nothing.

Perhaps they had decided that his gunfire was a thing they did not wish to face, no matter how contemptuous they were of his ability to shoot straight.

Then hope, which had been dead, sprang up into a giddy and instant life in him. He wormed his way rapidly back among the rocks until he had gained the crest of the little heap. And the first thing that he saw beneath him was a hat floating among the boulders, as though it rested on water!

He tried a snap shot hastily at that sombrero, and it disappeared at once.

A moment later a heavy slug beat against the fore head of a rock at Wayland's side. A stinging spray of lead whipped into his shoulder.

It merely grazed the skin, but the sting was as of hornets.

He withdrew to a little natural fortress at the top of the heap of rocks. Big boulders encircled, him. He could sit at ease and peer out through the gaps. But he saw nothing, he heard nothing. He had to look up to see a sign of life, where a pair of buzzards were circling high up. He wondered, with a cold thrill of awe, what information their devilish instincts had given to them, and how near a death might be. Not so very far away, the carcass of a horse was stretched for their feasting, but perhaps this pair preferred meat of a rarer sort.

After a while he began to grow very thirsty.

Thirst in dry Western air progresses rapidly from a

dryness of the throat to a fever of the brain. He hardly had noticed that he wanted a drink before he began to find it hard to swallow.

And the sun was still high up in the sky. But he controlled himself when the panic reached his mind. A man ought to be able to go two days without water, no matter what the heat. The prime necessity was to keep the nerves in hand.

That was easily said, not so easily done. As he sat there, broiling, he felt that the only thing that saved his stability was sight of a little green lizard with yellow markings along the back, that slid out on the surface of a rock and paused there, with its body still curved for the next whiplike movement and its head raised. It was so close that he could see the dim red flicker of the tongue now and then, and the glittering of the little eyes. The rock was hot enough to singe ordinary flesh, but that lizard was a true salamander. There was no hurry about it. If a day or two passed for it between insects—if a month or two intervened between drinks—what difference did it make?

Wayland began to smile and to forget about his own troubles.

That was how the afternoon sloped off into twilight. For all his spying, he had sight of nothing of interest except the two saddle horses, now grazing busily far up the floor of the canyon.

He had made up his mind by this time. He would wait not only until it was dark, but until the night had worn along for several hours. Then he would try to slip down among the boulders and get away. There would be no moon for some time to come.

In the meantime, the sky turned dim. A thin white cloud rolled into the west, the fires caught it, it blazed up and gave a false promise of a returning day. Then all went darker than ever. Suddenly the night was only a step away.

Wayland stood up to stretch himself. He stuck his arms up above his head, strained every muscle and tendon to the full, and heard the deep voice of Phil Bray saying, from behind:

"Keep 'em there!"

Wayland "kept them there."

As he stood with his hands high, suddenly it seemed to him that he had been the biggest fool in the world. He should have known in the beginning that one Wayland, with a burro, had no chance to escape from three accomplished desperadoes, well armed and mounted.

He heard Bray say: "All right, boys. I've got him here. Come up and get him for me. Wayland, don't stir none. Don't budge."

There were noises among the rocks. Then the lean, handsome face of Joe Mantry appeared. He stared at Wayland, full in the eyes, and remarked:

"Tag him out, chief. What's the use of' weighing ourselves down with him?"

"I dunno," said Bray. "I don't care much. How do you vote, Dave?"

Dave Lister got to the spot, breathing hard in his turn. He rested a sharp elbow against the side of a boulder as he murmured:

"Well, I dunno. We'll see what part of the loot he's got, first."

Bray said: "Open that saddlebag, Joe. Wayland, put your hands down behind your back. Put them down both at once, and keep still. I'd plug you for a nickel and a half."

Wayland believed him devoutly, and moved the

114

hands with exceeding care until they were in the small of his back, where they were grabbed and tied together by Bray. His gun was taken from him, too.

In the meantime, the other pair had opened the saddlebag and spilled out the contents. Joe Mantry was careful to a degree, counting. Dave Lister seemed able to note the contents with a glance.

He said suddenly: "Chief, it looks to me like we're not two hundred dollars short. And that's a fact!"

Bray sat on a rock, smoking a cigarette.

"It's getting pretty dark," he declared. "We'd better move on. What about our friend before we start?"

"Plug him," urged Mantry.

"There's a little reason in what you say," answered Bray. "This hombre seems to have a brain and a pair of hands about him. Listen, Wayland," he added. "How did you get this stuff?"

"I met your fourth man," answered Wayland. "I stuck him up with a gun. He got at me and started to work with his knife as I went down. He was slippery, but I managed to tap him on the right spot, and he went out. That's how I got hold of the money."

"What were you doing with it?" asked Bray.

"Well, I was heading back toward Elkdale."

"Elkdale? Why?"

"That's where the bank is, of course. I wanted to get it back into the safe."

"Hello!" murmured Bray. And he began to chuckle. "You would 'a' passed the wad all back to Old Man William Rucker, would you?"

"Sure he would. He's a nut, but he's no fool," observed Joe Mantry. "He had brains enough to get that slippery little devil of a Jimmy Lovell; he may have brains enough to stick to our trail, after we get the stuff,

115

and keep up long enough to give us away to a sheriff's posse."

"He *may* have the brains," commented Bray. "Boys, I don't care much. Only, we got the whole wad of the money back through this hombre. I say that it's too bad to look a gift horse in the face."

Dave Lister began to laugh softly. He picked up several of the thick wads of greenbacks and held them out to the faint evening light.

"There's enough to put the lot of us on Easy Street for a long time," he said. "Sure, chief. Get this hombre, this Wayland, out of the way. You know how it is. A crook is as weak as the weakest link in the chain, but an honest man is as strong as the strongest part of the chain."

Lister paused and laughed again to indicate that the words were not a belief with him. They were simply something that he had heard, and, therefore, that he was willing to repeat. People of his sort never really trust folklore or folk sayings, but they are always unwilling to close their ears to proverbial wisdom.

"Look," said Joe Mantry eagerly. "This fellow had the brains to snag Lovell. The rest of us couldn't wrangle that. He had the nerve to go and freeze himself to death above timber line, hunting for Lovell. And at last he got him. Make up your mind. You want him on our trail?"

"What makes you hate him so much? What's he done to you?" asked Bray.

The first dark of the night was doubly thick and close. Through it Mantry stepped close to the prisoner, until his face was only inches away.

"I hate his long, lean mug, if you want to know," said Mantry. "That's what I hate about him. Any objections,

116

anybody?"

He looked about him for a reply.

"You're going to get yourself a knife through you some day," said Phil Bray.

"Yeah? Who'll use the knife, then? Know his name?" asked Mantry in his most offensive manner.

"Maybe I'll use it myself," said Bray.

There was a sudden silence at this. The silence continued until it appeared that even the savage eagerness of Joe Mantry was not quite prepared to match itself against his leader.

Then Bray went on: "We gotta make up our minds. What about Wayland?"

"Well," said Mantry, "I've said my say. Speak the word, and I'll do the rest of it. I ain't afraid of ghosts."

Wayland's soul grew small in his breast. He waited. There was the voice of big Dave Lister to be heard, and Dave said:

"Well, the quicker the job, the sooner we'll have him off our hands, as far as I see it."

At that, Phil Bray answered suddenly: "I dunno. You don't want to look a gift horse in the mouth; anybody knows that. It spoils your luck for you. Anybody here that wants to be out of luck?"

There was no answer.

"We're not going to run all day and all night with him," went on Bray. "We gotta camp somewhere and plan things out. He could stay with us a while, and we wouldn't be losing any time. How about that?"

"If you come across a whole orphanage," said bitter young Joe Mantry, "you'd take the whole shooting match along with you to rob a bird's nest. You've made up your mind. You'll take Wayland along with you. But mind you—hell is going to pop!"

117

"What makes you think that?"

"I feel it in my bones," answered Mantry. "I'll crack his head for him, and we'll roll a few rocks over him. He picked this place out for his grave, didn't he? He wanted a monument on the spot, didn't he?"

Mantry laughed as he completed his suggestion. And still Phil Bray shook his head.

"Mantry has a hunch, chief. Let him have his own way," urged Lister.

Bray said: "Not now. We'll talk it over later on. I wouldn't want to see this poor fool socked on the head. Not now. We'll talk it over later on."

In that casual manner, at the last moment, the life of Wayland was spared. But he knew that death was still in the very air that he breathed.

THE DOUBLE CROSS

BRAY CHOSE THE CAMP, AND IN AN ODD PLACE. HE selected a hillside slope and a big clearing. Through the clearing ran a swift, shallow stream of snow water. There were a few bushes near by, but the trees all stood back a considerable distance. The exact spot where Bray chose to build the camp fire was where a number of rocks cropped out from the ground.

Joe Mantry took serious exception to the site. He said: "All that a man hunter would need to do would be to lie down on the edge of the trees and snipe at us. We're all right out here in the open. We're held up to view. It's a cinch for anybody that's after us. Jimmy Lovell, say."

Bray answered: "Well, they'll have nothing much to shoot by, considering the distance. Look at the fire."

118

It was a small flame, just enough to heat coffee and broil some rabbit meat.

"Look at the shadows," went on Bray.

In fact, as the flame swayed this way and that, the shadows thrown by the rocks wavered also through the air, and no perceptible light reached the trees.

"Come back, all of you, and take a look from the edge of the trees," went on Bray.

Accordingly, they all retreated to the verge of the woods. From that viewpoint the camp seemed secure indeed. Even the big bodies of the horses were wavering and obscure in the sweep of the shadows, as though they were objects afloat in the water. The rocks themselves, it was apparent, were perfect breastworks behind which the party could take shelter.

"Besides," said Bray, "there ain't much chance that we'll be sniped at. Suppose that Lovell got on the trail. It ain't blood that he wants, but the money. He'd try to sneak-thieve the coin again, and that's all there is to it. And we've got a place here where the horses get enough good grazing. We've got water at our feet. And with one man on guard, I wanta ask you how anything but a mole or a bird could get at us? Anybody answer up?"

To this there was a silence, and Dave Lister actually bent back his head and looked up into the air, as though expecting that danger might at that moment be coming toward them on the wing.

They went back to the camp, and the cooking started. Lister drew the lot as the first guard, and began to stalk back and forth, on the alert.

Jimmy Lovell, they all admitted, was a clever fellow, but it was considered that the problem of getting at them in such an encampment as this would be totally beyond his powers.

The hopes of Wayland, in the meantime, gradually diminished. Finally they reached zero, for it seemed clear that there was nothing for him to do except pray that his own life might be saved from the trouble in which he stood.

Phil Bray still adopted an attitude of kindness. The hands of Wayland were freed, and, under strict guard, he was permitted to eat his share of the food and drink some coffee. He was even allowed to smoke a cigarette, and while he was smoking it, Joe Mantry opened the conversation again:

"It's a queer thing that Lovell would pick out Iron Mountain. How come?"

"Yeah, I been thinking about that," admitted Bray. "It beats me, too!"

He was puffing at a short-stemmed pipe so hard that the glow of the coal kept illumining his face in short pulsations of light.

"It wouldn't seem nacheral," said Bray, "for an hombre like Lovell to stay put with his wad of coin. Not after he knew that we were loose and on his trail. Seems more like he would keep drifting and pretty soon break right out of the mountains and clear away. Did you talk to him, Wayland?"

"I talked to him," said Wayland. "I've got an idea why he stays on Iron Mountain."

"Why?" snapped Mantry.

"Well, he says that he has a friend on Iron Mountain who would take care of him if anything happened."

"A friend? What, you mean one man?" asked Bray.

"Yes," said Wayland, and nodded thoughtfully. He was beginning to see a vague hope of a way out for himself.

"One man to guard Lovell against the three of us?

Jimmy ain't such a fool as all of that," remarked Joe Mantry. "He wouldn't trust any one man in the world to guard him against all of us. Not even Jim Silver, that Bray is always talking about."

"Well," said Wayland, "he has a man that he trusts, just the same. He wasn't very worried because I got the money away from him. He said that his friend would follow along and get it back from me."

"What friend?" asked Bray shortly.

Wayland smiled. "Boys," he said, "you know how it is. I naturally want to do all I can for you. But the rule in business is that you never do something for nothing."

"You hear that?" asked Mantry, turning his handsome head toward Bray.

"I hear it," said Bray. "Blame him?"

"I'd cut his throat for him if he didn't talk out!" observed Mantry.

"A cut throat doesn't say a lot, either," answered Bray. "But maybe there's nothing behind all of this." He said to Wayland: "You stringing us along, Wayland?"

Wayland shook his head.

"Come out with it, then," said Bray.

"It's worth a bargain, what I could tell you," said Wayland.

"Joe," ordered Bray, "try a hand at making him talk."

"I'll try a hand, all right," said Joe Mantry.

He got to his feet and brought a gun into his hand. He stepped over to Wayland and put the gun against his head.

"Now, you talk pronto," he said, "or I'll blow you into a deep sleep. I'll be the sandman for you. I'll close your eyes for you!"

Wayland looked up at the savage face of Mantry. By the tremor of the gun that was pressed against his temple, he could feel the wild desire to kill that was in Mantry. But there was in Wayland, at bottom, a calmly invincible stubbornness of character.

"No," he said to Mantry calmly.

"You hear that, chief?" snarled Mantry. And by the tightening of his face, Wayland knew that Mantry's finger was tightening on the trigger also.

"Wait a minute, Joe," put in Bray.

"Yeah, I knew that you'd spoil it," said Mantry, stepping back with a curse. "I was going to soften him up so that he'd take fingerprints, was all. Now you've spoiled it."

"You'd 'a' softened him up till he was dead," said Bray, "and the fact is that even Joe Mantry is old enough to know that dead men can't talk."

"All the better," said Mantry.

"Unless you want to hear what they know," replied Bray. "And I want to hear what Wayland knows."

Dave Lister broke in suddenly as he came to a halt in his pacing:

"I want to know, too. That bird has something in his crop."

"What's your price?" asked Bray.,

"You turn me loose," said Wayland.

"Not on your life!" answered Mantry.

"I dunno," said Lister. "Why not? What's the good of dragging this guy around with us? And if we slam him, we're marking off our trail with red. And that's no business, either."

"Wayland," said Bray suddenly, "you'll get what you want, then. Tell us about the friend of Lovell?"

"His name is Jim Silver," said Wayland.

Bray got up to his feet. He took the pipe out of his mouth and made a gesture that sent the ashes from the

122

bowl flying out into a thin arc that hung an instant in the air.

"Silver?" he muttered. "Jim Silver?"

"That's what Lovell told me."

"Jim Silver?" echoed Dave Lister. "Then Silver will come down on our trail!"

"Steady," said Joe Mantry. "You gents make me sick—Silver's only flesh and blood, and he can't see in the dark. We're safe enough here till the morning. And if he sees us then, why, we'll have a chance to see him, too, and if three can shoot as well as one, maybe we'll nail that hombre and put an end to him!"

He spoke with a rising confidence, so that it was plain that the need of a fight was in his blood.

"We'll stay here till morning," said Bray slowly. He put the pipe back between his teeth and gritted them against the stem of it. "And then, in the morning," he went on, "we'll start trekking. We'll split up the coin, and we'll head every man for a different point on the compass."

He fell silent again.

"What's the main idea?" said Dave Lister, his voice running up sharp and high. "Split up in a pinch?"

"Because," said Bray, "if he finds us all together, he'll swallow us all at a bite. We've got no chance against him. But if we scatter, probably two of us will get away. One of us is pretty sure to, by traveling fast and keeping on going."

"You're that afraid of him, are you?" asked Joe Mantry, sneering again.

Bray looked at him with a vague eye.

"Don't talk to me, Joe," he said. "I've got to think."

He sat down again, and was buried in thought. Then Wayland said:

"All right, boys. I've lived up to my side of the bargain. I'll go now. I'm not afraid of the dark."

Bray did not seem to hear, but Mantry laughed loudly. He crossed to Wayland, and, with a jab of his foot, drew attention.

"You poor fool," he said, "we told you that we'd turn you loose, but we didn't tell you when! You'll stay put till we're ready to handle you."

Wayland stared at Bray, and the big man gave him no heed. He looked toward Dave Lister, and saw the tall fellow grinning as he strode back and forth.

There was no use in appealing to either of them, he understood. The double cross was perfectly apparent. There was nothing for Wayland to do but stare at the fire and wonder how many hours separated him from the death that would now surely come. He knew too much, and he had revealed too much. They would have to get rid of him. That swiftly running stream of snow water might be the answer.

FOLLOWING FROSTY

IT HAD SEEMED TO JIMMY LOVELL THAT HE WOULD never be able to set Silver in motion, but once that famous man had commenced to act, Lovell felt that all he needed to do was to sit back and take things easy. In the first place, he would merely bring Jim Silver to the place where he had last seen Wayland. Then he would simply watch Silver work.

"But it's going to be dark," wailed Lovell. "It's going to be dark before long, and then you can't do anything."

"You show me the place where you met him," said Silver, and mounted Parade.

124

At the same time there was a rustling sound in the brush, and Frosty came bounding out at them. There was enough light to show thin streaks of blood on his vest, and it was plain that even in this short absence the matchless hunter had managed to find food. When he saw his master on Parade, he sat down and pointed his nose at the man and ruffed out his mane. Lovell set himself to withstand the ghostly sound of the wolf howl. But it did not come.

Lovell was on his mustang by this time. They had broken camp in a very few minutes, because a Jim Silver camp never had many things lying about. A wolf can pause where it pleases and curl up for sleep, and Jim Silver seemed to be able to do the same thing.

So Lovell led the way down the slope to the spot where he had last seen Wayland.

The day was nearly dead now, but out of the ground, lingering on the grass, there seemed to rise a thin luster. The dew was not yet falling, but the gleam of the green was as though it were wet.

Lovell pointed out the important features. Here he had ridden the horse; here he had shot the rabbit; there Wayland had stood among the trees; there he had stalked out here he had confronted Lovell; there they had wrestled on the ground, there where the crushed grass was slowly erecting itself again; and, finally, in these places the little burro had gone away, with its master following after him.

While this explanation took place, Silver kept Parade and the wolf at a distance. As it ended, he brought in Frosty with a gesture and showed him first the impressions of the feet of Wayland, letting him fill his nostrils with the scent. Afterward he picked up the bail of the burro. Then he mounted.

125

It was deep twilight now, and Frosty struck off along that trail at a steady lope that kept the horses at a trot or a canter. Only now and then the wolf paused, scented right and left, or threw his muzzle high into the air, and then went rapidly on again.

Another picture came suddenly into the mind of Lovell—of himself fleeing for life, and this relentless pursuer following over a trail that the eyes of no man could hold, with Parade striding in the rear, and Jim Silver and his guns mounted on the stallion. It was a partnership, Lovell felt, of more than human power. Dread made his scalp prickle, and anger worked in his heart. Even while Silver was laboring for him, Lovell felt a finer hatred distilling in his soul.

They got into rough country, where it was difficult to follow the wolf by sight, for the gray of his coat seemed to fit into the color of the shrubbery and of the rocks. He glided like a vanishing thought before them.

Even then Lovell did not have to worry. For Parade would follow Frosty by the scent, easily. So, blindly conducted, Lovell went forward, his mustang on a constant lope now, until they were journeying up a big canyon with a flat floor. In the midst of this Frosty stopped. Parade halted a moment later beside him, snorting softly, and stamping.

"Something strange," said Silver, "but probably it's not dangerous. Frosty won't go closer unless I lead him in."

He rode Parade forward a short distance, then turned in a moment and called:

"The body of a dead horse. That's all. But there's one strange thing about it. The saddle and bridle are still on it!"

"Somebody was in a hurry. How did it die?" asked

126

Lovell.

Silver was already on the ground, lighting a match. Lovell did not even dismount. It was useless, he felt, to add his acute observation to the all-seeing eyes of Jim Silver.

"Shot," said Silver. "A rifle bullet at fairly long range."

He dropped the match. His stern face disappeared in the night once more. Again Lovell had the strange, shuddering feeling that this man was pursuing *him*, not Wayland.

Frosty, in the meantime, had slipped up to the dead carcass, sniffed at the saddle, and now uttered a faint howl and started on back trail.

"He's afraid!" exclaimed Lovell.

"Not afraid. He's telling us that our man left this horse and went back down the canyon."

"But Wayland had a burro, not a horse!"

"Well, if he wanted a horse, he had money enough with him to buy it, I suppose."

"Or he might steal it. And then somebody started shooting at him?"

Silver had lighted another match and with it was running back up the canyon floor in the direction from which the dead horse had evidently been coming. Parade, his mane and the reins of his hackamore tossing, followed his master closely. But Frosty remained in the distance, sitting down and watching Silver's proceedings. There in the starlight, the big wolf looked like a dim ghost.

Silver had lighted several more matches. Now he mounted Parade and returned to Lovell.

He reported: "That horse was traveling on a dead run. A bullet hit it. It began to sag. Its strides shortened back there. The rider dismounted and ran on ahead. That rider was Wayland, or Frosty would not be so keen to follow him. Come on!"

Silver called. The wolf once more sprang out on the invisible trail, and passing down the ravine for a short distance, he then made a sharp turn to the right, into the black mouth of a narrow valley. Silver whistled. Frosty went on at a skulking walk until they came out of the utter blackness of that entrance into a wider valley inside. Before them they saw the dim outlines of a rocky hummock.

Silver dismounted at once.

"That's the sort of a place that a man might use as a fort," he said. "I'm going to take a look at it."

Take a look at it, thought Lovell, in the black of the night, not knowing what danger or desperate men might be concealed? He himself remained well to the rear while Silver ran ahead with Frosty. They slowed as they came near to the rocks. Then they disappeared from view.

Lovell gradually let his mustang drift in pursuit. And after a moment, Silver and the wolf came in sight, once more, rounding the side of the hummock. Silver mounted Parade; Frosty turned off to the side.

"More than one trail goes away from here," said Silver. "Only one trail came up to it, so far as we know. Now watch Frosty go through the night!"

The wolf, in fact, no longer held to any settled direction, but repeatedly shifted to this side and to that, eventually settling down on one trail, as it appeared.

When the pursuers came to a place where the grass was thin and the ground soft, Silver dismounted again, and lighted more matches. His survey was quickly made.

128

He said, as he remounted: "The line that Frosty is following is that of a man on foot. There are two men on foot, in fact. And there are two horse trails through the grass. Three men, and they've got Wayland. Three men that he ran away from, I suppose."

"Three?" cried Lovell, in an agony of excitement and of fear.

"That's the way I make it. Is three the right number?"

"They've got him," groaned Lovell. "They'll slit his gullet and take the coin. Listen to me, Jim Silver. You're the fellow that's famous for doing right by innocent men. Well, here's a good chance for you. Here's Wayland. He's innocent, all right. He's never done any harm—except to me—and now three of the worst thugs in the world have him. They've cut his throat by this time—if they have half the brains that they used to own. He's a dead man. There's my money to get back, and there's the blood of an honest man on this trail. You hear, Silver? Does that make you cock your ears?"

Silver laid nothing at all, for a moment, Then he asked:

"Are the three of them cronies of yours? Old cronies that you've broken with?"

"They're a flock of jailbirds," said Lovell savagely.

"Well," said Silver, "you've been in prison yourself, I've seen."

"What makes you say that?"

"There's a down twist to the mouth and a way of whispering that men learn only from a few years of the lock step," said Silver.

"I don't talk like that," exclaimed Lovell.

"No, you don't talk like that. But when you're thinking a thing out, you *whisper* to yourself that way."

129

A bubbling sound arose in the throat of Lovell. He thanked his stars that Jim Silver had not reached out a hand for him, no matter from what distance. All possibilities of conversation were dried up in the throat of Lovell. He could merely gasp out:

"I tell you, Silver, even if you can see in the dark, the way some people say that you can, you'll certainly have your hands full with the three of 'em."

"Ay, but there's you, Lovell," said Silver dryly. "You'll be up there in the thick of the fight, I suppose."

"Me?" snarled Lovell. "I'll put a tooth in 'em if I get a good chance—but my way might not be your way. You've got to remember that."

"True," said Silver. "We may have different ways of going about things."

He led on, following Frosty, for the wolf had now disappeared in the trees and was traveling up the mountainside. Presently Frosty led them in a small detour, and they found him, half faded into the shadows, erect, with head thrown high.

"He's lost the scent!" groaned Lovell. "The fool has brought us all this way and lost the scent for us!"

"He's taking it out of the wind instead of off the ground," answered Silver softly. "Dismount, and walk on your toes. Don't rustle as much as a blade of grass. We're close to whatever trouble we're going to have. Tether that mustang, unless it can move the way Parade does."

But what other horse could move as Parade moved in a time of danger? What other by years of a wild, free life, and then by long training with such a master, had learned to drift through a forest as silently as the great moose that goes in and out of the northern woods like a strange image of the mind?

Lovell tied the mustang and followed on foot, until he saw before him, through the trees, the vague shudder and tremor and lifting of shadows around a small camp fire. He knew then that he was coming close to the great moment.

IN THE BANDITS' CAMP

HERE ON THE VERGE OF THE TREES THE TWO OF THEM paused. The whole scene was decipherable, though the tone of it was very dull and low. The waver of the flame of the camp fire cast as much confusion as light. But they could see the three seated near the fire, one with his hands bound behind him, and they could mark the figure that walked back and forth on guard.

"They have brains," said Silver. "They know how to choose a camp, and that's the most important knowledge that a man can have—for this sort of a business!"

"If we take the guns," murmured Lovell, "we could pick 'em off!"

"We could kill or hurt a pair of 'em," said Silver quietly. "But that's no good. I don't even know that they need killing."

"You don't know? Ain't I told you that they're all a lot of thugs?" demanded Lovell.

"You've told me that," answered Silver shortly.

Lovell was silent. His hatred of Silver waxed a little greater in the interval of pause.

"That other one—with his arms tied—is that the fellow who stopped you and took the saddlebags?"

"I can't make out his face. Yes, that must be Wayland."

"If we start shooting and the three of them are thugs, they'll slit Wayland's throat for him before they answer our fire. We can't bombard them from a distance."

"It'd be a lot more polite if we went up and introduced ourselves first and asked them for the saddlebag," said Lovell, with his sneer.

"Yes," said Silver absently, "that would be more polite."

Lovell's whisper screamed high against his palate:

"What are you talking about? Silver, those three are all out of the pen. They're out of the death house. You'd be *admired* for killing them! Robbery and murder in Elkdale. They've all gotta swing for it."

"Is that money in the saddlebag," said Silver, "is that part of the Elkdale loot?"

Lovell was silent, but his breathing could be heard. His distress was more eloquent than words could make it.

Silver permitted the silence, and at last he said "There are three thugs, over there—three fellows out of the death house—poor devils! And Wayland. You say that Wayland is a thug, too?"

"He's got no more right to the money than I have!" said Lovell. "It's mine!"

"Is Wayland an honest man?" asked Silver.

"The fool ain't got the sense to be anything else!" snarled the whisper of Lovell.

He saw Silver turn a little toward him, as though the last words had a peculiar weight in the mind of the big man.

"Wait here," said Silver. "I'm going to explore." He pulled the reins over the head of Parade and let them hang. Then he disappeared among the trees to the left.

He was gone during one of the longest half hours in

132

the life of Lovell. During that time, the tall man who had been striding back and forth and who must have been Dave Lister, went back beside the fire and lay down. A smaller guard took up the rounds, stepping with a quick and light movement, his head alert and uneasy as he walked. That would be Joe Mantry. Lovell felt that he could tell the step of the man-killer by his silhouette—tell it in an army of others.

The whole trio by the camp fire had now disappeared by the rocks. Perhaps they were already asleep when a shadow stirred near Lovell and he saw a slinking form and the green, phosphorescent light of the eyes of a beast of prey. Another form loomed immediately behind. It was Silver and Frosty, of course. And a shudder that was beginning to be familiar in the body of Lovell, like an accustomed nightmare, ran through his flesh.

Silver said: "I'm going to try to get at the camp."

"You might as well try to walk up to a tiger in broad daylight," said Lovell. "That gent who's walking on guard *is* a tiger. Lemme tell you something, Silver. You're famous for gun work, but at your best you never were no better than Joe Mantry."

"I'm going to try to get at the camp," answered Silver calmly. "You go back to where we left your horse, and move it over to the creek's bank. Come up the bank slowly, toward the camp. If you hear an outbreak of voices and shooting, you'll know that I've been spotted. If you hear my whistle and the noise of a horse, you'll know that I've gotten to Parade. But this is going to be work. I'm trying to get the stolen money. I'm trying to get Wayland, too."

"Trying to get Wayland? Silver, don't be a fool and—"

"Do what I tell you," said Silver. "And if I get

133

Wayland free, then there will be three against three, and I suppose we may be able to handle them."

Handle them? Yes, but first how could Jim Silver reach that well-posted, well-guarded camp?

The very soul of Lovell was consumed with curiosity.

But Silver, tossing the reins back over the pommel of the stallion's saddle, went off, followed by the horse, preceded by the gliding ghost, Frosty. They faded silently into the woods, and Lovell turned back to, get to his own mustang.

He felt a vague content. Whatever happened, there would be trouble for both Silver and the three. If they slaughtered one another to the last man, it would be perfectly pleasing to Lovell. He would almost give up his hope of the money for the sake of such an ending to his schemes.

Silver brought the big horse close to the bank of the stream. There, where a thicket of brush grew densely as cover, he left Parade again and posted Frosty, with a whisper, to guard the big horse. Then he returned in a wide semi-circle through the woods to the opposite side of the clearing.

He had very little time, for the moon was about to rise, he knew. At his side, down a shallow bank, ran the road that he was to follow to the camp. It was the coldly flickering stream of snow water.

He took off his boots and tied them, together with his guns, about his neck. Those well-oiled guns and the ammunition in them would defy the effect of water for a short time, at least. And whatever he did would have to be consummated rapidly.

So he, entered the water.

It was so cold that the first touch of it seared his flesh like fire. Yet he lay down in the current. It was rapid

134

and whirling, but so shallow that his hands could touch the bottom most of the way. And that sliding stream bore him now down toward the camp of the three and their fortune in stolen money, and their captured man.

He let the current bear him until he saw a dull red flicker of light across the surface. Then he pulled himself out until his head and shoulders were free of the stream.

He was so cold that he knew that he was nearly helpless. A child of ten could have handled him, frozen as he was. And yet he was approaching a threefold danger.

"Man-killer," Lovell had called Joe Mantry. And the catlike quickness and lightness of the steps of Mantry, as he walked back and forth on guard, made Silver confident that Lovell had not misnamed his man.

He could see Mantry now, moving rapidly, pausing an instant each time he came to the end of his beat. Merely the sound of the water that was running, now, out of the clothes of Silver, seemed sufficient to attract the attention of such an ear.

But Silver was able to drag himself clear of the water, unheeded, and so like a snake to twist and wriggle himself forward until he was inside the nest of rocks.

There was still both flame and spreading heat from the camp fire. The heat itself was a blessing to Silver. He had a great, mad impulse to rise to his knees, guns in hand, and murder sleeping men, so that he could safely extend his arms around that fire and be warmed to the core of his heart.

One man lay on his back, with lean, long face looking as pale as stone. Another lay with his head resting on his saddle and looking very uncomfortable. But he was snoring softly, regularly in his sleep. Silver blessed that noise of snoring. It might cover a thousand other guilty noises of his own making, before long.

The third man was the prisoner. He was tall, also, and even in sleep, Silver thought that he could see pain and resolution in the face of Wayland.

With all his heart he was ready to believe what Lovell had said—that this was an honest man.

He crawled closer until he could whisper in the ear of the prisoner:

"Wake up but don't move. Wake up but don't move. Wake up but keep still."

He kept repeating that over and over. And finally there was a little tremor that ran through the body of Wayland. He opened his eyes and heard:

"Wake up, but don't stir."

He did not stir. He merely rolled his eyes and saw the body of the man beside him, the wet clothing faintly glimmering in the starlight, and by the uncertain rays of the flickering fire.

He raised his head a little and was able to see, at last, that the stranger was shuddering in an ague fit with the intensity of cold. His hands were unsteady. His head strained back on his neck. His wet face was red as blood.

Yet there was no disguising the features.

Suddenly the mind of Wayland went back to that other day when he had so calmly nailed up the picture of Jim Silver and Parade on the wall of the bank, to bring home to every man working there the example of a hero, unafraid to stand for the right thing.

Had not the thought of that same face forced him, perhaps, to take up the uncertainties of this trail, when he dared to match his wits against the bandits? For the sake of what Silver stood for in the world, Wayland had tried to act the part of a hero—and won in exchange the probability of an obscure death the next morning.

But he had won something else. Jim Silver in person was there to succor him.

He saw the gleam of Silver's knife. He felt the light pull at the cords as the knife edge sheared through them. And then his hands were free.

They were free, but almost helpless. He moved them toward the saddlebag which still contained every penny of the treasure.

Bray had said: "Use this for your pillow, Wayland. Maybe it'll give you happy dreams, eh?"

Bray had grinned, making that sardonic remark, and Wayland had remained awake for a time wondering how they would kill him—knife or gun. Or perhaps savage Joe Mantry would be able to devise some better scheme. He was a man of devices, was Joe Mantry.

The whisper of Silver said: "Give me the bag. Follow me!"

Wayland passed the saddlebag over, readily. There was no other man in the world that he would have rendered it to, but he had not an instant's misgiving.

Then he saw a warning gesture from Silver, and observed the man collapse suddenly along the ground. Wayland did the same. He even had sufficient presence of mind to push his numbed arms behind his back and so he lay with the terrible consciousness that a head and shoulders loomed above the rocks against the stars.

Joe Mantry had come to look at the group inside the nest of rocks. If he gave a casual glance, all might be well. If he used his wits, he could not fail to make out the bleared outlines of four forms instead of three.

A shudder of electric fire filled the brain of Wayland—and then he saw the silhouette disappear!

Silver's whisper reached him at the same instant, saying: "Follow me. Down into the water after me."

And he saw the body of Silver slide down noiselessly into the stream.

He followed, as cautiously as he could.

The cold seized him. The fingers of ice laid hold on his bones. And then the force of the water carried him rapidly forward, while with his hands on the bottom he tried to ease' his way.

A projecting rock struck him heavily on the chest. He gasped. Water entered his throat and half strangled him. Instinctively he rose from the shallow stream and fell forward again into the water with a loud splashing.

Voices were shouting, instantly, behind him, and a gun began to fire rapidly.

FLAMING GUNS

HE DIVED FORWARD AGAIN INTO THE ICY STREAM. ITS cold meant nothing to him now. Vaguely, before him, he saw the shadows of the brush. He rose again and stumbled toward it, as though its arms could shield him even from bullets.

He saw the big body of Silver rise from the water, also, and felt the hand of Silver catch him and drag him into the brush. Looking back, he saw fire spitting from three guns, near the camp. Those points of light winked closer and closer as the three began to run forward. At the same time, he heard the sound of a muffled, heavy blow, and Jim Silver lunged forward and struck the ground.

Wayland could not realize what had happened. Silver was a fact in the world as indestructible, as permanent as the mountains. Mere powder and lead could not, it seemed, do him harm. And yet now he lay there motionless on the ground!

The saddlebag with the loot in it had tumbled across the body of the fallen man. And he, Wayland, had been the clumsy fool who had drawn the attention of Joe Mantry to the flight.

There was one wild impulse in Wayland to snatch up the saddlebag and flee for his life with the treasure. Then he saw the body on the ground stir, and the madness left his brain.

He caught one of Silver's guns, and standing straight, he opened fire on the three forms That were lacing toward him. Over the tips of the bushes he could see them scatter to right and left suddenly, and disappear in the woods.

At the same time, a thin whistle sounded from the ground. That was Silver giving a call that was answered by a great rushing, and Parade dashed up through the brush with Frosty beside him.

A gasping voice came from Silver and the stallion slumped to the ground beside him.

"Get me into the saddle. Parade will carry double. Get me into the saddle, Wayland!" breathed the voice of Silver.

Wayland, shuddering with dread, laid his hands and all his strength on the wounded man. And still his brain would not admit that this helpless bulk of flesh could be Jim Silver. But Silver it was, and the great horse that had kneeled like an Arab's camel was Parade, and the green-eyed monster that snarled softly, close to them, was Frosty, the wolf.

So Wayland worked the burden of Silver's almost inert body onto the back of the horse.

He heard Bray, calling: "Joe, go back for horses. Dave, come on with me. Cut in toward the bank of the creek. We'll get 'em. Shoot at anything you see. Hell is loose in the air!"

Instantly there was the explosion of a gun, and a bullet clattered through the branches close to Wayland's head.

He thought, for an instant, that he had been seen and was a visible target, but the shot was not repeated for another moment. And in the meantime, Parade had lunged to his feet.

Wayland swung up behind the wounded man. To manage the saddlebag with one hand and grip the body of Silver with the other was all that he could do. He had to leave Parade to his own head, and that seemed, after all, the better way.

For the big horse wound rapidly through the brush, dodged among the trees, and came out in the open floor of a valley just beyond.

In the east, there was a growing pyramid of yellow, pale light to tell where the moon was about to rise. Behind them, in the woods, voices were calling out more dimly.

They had escaped safely, it seemed. But what did the escape mean if the life of Jim Silver were running momentarily out of his body?

"Lift me up. Help me," commanded the murmur of Silver.

Wayland used his strength to lift up the torso of the wounded man. And the bulk of Silver lolled heavily back against him. A shadowy horseman swept out from the right and made straight toward them. Wayland leveled a revolver at the right.

"Steady!" said Silver: "It's not one of the three. It's

140

Lovell. He's with us against the others, no matter what sort of a rat he is. Wayland, get me across the valley and into the trees. Leave me there. Go on with Lovell. Get yourselves away from danger, quick!"

Get across the valley into the opposite trees—leave Jim Silver—save themselves?

The mustang of Lovell drew up beside them as Parade struck forward with a long, easy canter.

"The saddlebag?" he called. "Did you get it?"

"Silver's hurt," said Wayland. "Watch out behind us. Silver's hurt!"

"That's his luck," cried Lovell. "Have you got the bag? I see it. Here, give it to me. I'll take care of it! We'll pull together, partner!"

The hungry cupidity of Lovell made Wayland almost smile.

He shouted in answer: "They're coming! Follow on Lovell!"

For far behind them they could distinctly hear the beat of hoofs and the crashing of brush as riders drove their horses recklessly through the woods. And as Parade increased his pace, throwing up his head and half turning it, as though inquiring after the state of his master, as Frosty began to labor his best to keep up with the long-striding stallion, Lovell fell cursing behind the leader.

They swept across the valley. They were entering the edge of the opposite forest when Wayland heard the loud yell of men tingling out of the distance—Indian yells of triumph—and he knew that the three had sight of their quarry.

He estimated their strength quickly. Silver would be of no use for fighting, probably. That left Lovell, who would be a treacherous companion, to say the best. And as for himself, Wayland knew that he was a very poor shot.

Against him and the doubtful quantity of Lovell there were ranged the adroit shrewdness of Dave Lister, the panther-like ferocity and killing instinct of Joe Mantry, and above all the more capacious and patient strength of Philip Bray.

What could the fugitives do? Even Parade could not carry double for an indefinite time. And the moon was rising now, to show the way to the pursuit.

The light from the east threw long, slanting shadows among the trees.

Now, as they labored up the slope of the hill, Silver was saying:

"You can let me down anywhere. Frosty'll stay with me. If you give Parade his head, he may be willing to carry you away from me. I don't know. I hope he will. Give him his head, and he may keep on with Lovell's horse. But if you try to rein him and control him, he'll fight you till he kills you or you kill him. Let me down anywhere—and run for your lives!"

Run for their lives, and leave Jim Silver dying there among the shadows of the trees?

"Save your breath," said Wayland shortly. "I'm not leaving you, Silver, no matter what happens."

"You fool!" whispered Silver weakly.

Up from the rear came the struggling mustang of Lovell. And Lovell's voice called:

"Silver, are you hurt?"

"He's badly hurt. We've got to pull up and fight it out with the three of 'em," said Wayland. "Silver's out of it. He's fought enough for other people. Now we've got a chance to fight for him!"

Lovell reined his horse closer and leaned far out from

142

the saddle to peer at the limp form of Silver, and suddenly he exclaimed:

"He's got it! He's done for! Silver's gone!"

Gone? Well, perhaps he was. With a sick heart, Wayland had been feeling the trickling of hot blood out of the body of Jim Silver. Jim Silver apparently was dying, and it was plain that Lovell was far from displeased.

"He can't lift a hand!" said Lovell. "Pass me the saddlebag, Wayland. I'll carry it for you: I'll stick with you, too. The pair of us, we'll get clear. We'll fight our way through."

They had climbed up the slope through the woods until they came to a canyon that gave them, for a moment, easier footing, and now they were passing many small, dark mouths of side cuts that sliced back from the main throat of the ravine.

"We'll take him in here," said Wayland, and they came to a long and narrow cleft that promised to run back for a considerable distance through the mountain. "We'll take him in here. They've got no noses to follow our scent, and maybe they won't be able to follow the trail with their eyes till morning."

"You fool," cried Lovell, "they'll just bottle us up, in there! Let Silver drop. He's done for a lot of others, and now his turn has come. Let him drop, and come along with me. Man, we've got half a million to ride for. Are you going to throw us away on a dead one?"

But Wayland already had swerved big Parade to the side, with a swing of his body, and they were passing straight back into the close, thick darkness of the ravine.

THE RAVINE

THE VOICE OF JIM SILVER, PITCHED VERY LOW, murmured at the ear of Wayland like soundless thought rising in his own mind: "Let me down. You've done enough. I know that your heart's right. No use throwing yourself away when you can't really help me."

"Listen," said Wayland, for he felt himself weakening under the steady flow of Silver's persuasion. "Listen to me. It was me being a clumsy fool that brought you into the trouble. You came to save my neck. You could have had the saddlebag for the taking, but you took me along, too. And then I blundered and got Mantry's eye, and *you* absorbed the bullet that should have been for me. Now you tell me to run off and leave you alone. Well, I won't run off. Don't persuade me. It's hard enough for me to try to do what's right without arguing about it."

A glint of stronger moonlight was reflected from the shining face of a cliff of quartz, and by that strange light, Wayland saw the eyes of Silver had closed and that his pale lips were smiling a little.

"All right," said Silver. "It's better to die like a white man than to keep on living like a sneak. I won't argue any more."

"We're going to cut through this ravine. We're going to get out on the high ground and bed you down in a corner where Bray and the rest will never find you. We're going to stop your bleeding. And a month from now, you and I will be in Elkdale eating beefsteak and laughing about the scare we're going through now."

That optimistic speech had hardly stopped sounding from the lips of Wayland when they turned a corner and found that the canyon pitched out to nothing, suddenly. Straight before them there was a slope of seventy degrees or more. It went up and up, endlessly, to the very peak of the mountain.

It might be that Parade could climb that slope alone. But it, was certain that he could never manage it with a man on his back.

Wayland halted the horse and looked helplessly around him. Lovell appeared, fuming, groaning, talking low as though he feared the enemy were already in hearing distance.

"You see what you've done? You've bottled us up!" he gasped. "I never heard of such a fool. Bottled up two living gents and one dead one and half a million dollars of good, clean money!"

"Watch him!" whispered Silver to Wayland. "Watch his guns!"

Wayland slipped suddenly out of the saddle and put Parade between him and Lovell.

"I'm taking Silver off the horse," he said. "Watch the mouth of the ravine. We'll talk things over. We'll try to find a way out, man!"

He took the weight of Silver over his shoulder, as he spoke, and lowered him from the saddle. Silver stood beside him, one loose, big arm cast over the shoulders of Wayland, and his head sagging down. The tremor of his weakness Wayland could feel. And the irregular breathing of Silver told of the pain that he was enduring.

Off to the side, there was a sort of natural penthouse, where the bottom of the rock gave back. And into this, Wayland supported Silver and stretched him on the ground.

Lovell followed, still arguing, but Wayland had slung the saddlebag over his shoulder and now he dropped it between the prostrate form of Silver and the rock wall.

Lovell said, his voice whining as he strove to make it persuasive: "We going to throw ourselves away for a dead man. We're going to—"

"Wait," said Wayland. "I'm not fool enough to throw myself away for a dead man. We'll tie up his wound. That's all. We'll tie him up and see how he is: Then we'll talk. Give me a hand, Lovell!"

"And waste the time that might save our necks—and half a million dollars. I tell you, it ain't right to throw away a chunk of coin like that!"

But he fell to, with his little, rapid hands, to make bare the wound of Silver.

The slug had torn right through his body. The mark where it entered, under the breast, was comparatively small. But there was a great hole in the back. Certainly it seemed that there was no way of keeping the life from flying out through such an aperture. Wayland turned sick as, by the dim moonlight, he saw the truth of things.

"You see?" snapped Lovell.

"We'll just tie him up!" urged Wayland.

"Oh, well—" said Jimmy Lovell through his teeth.

But he helped, nevertheless. With dust they stopped the mouths of the wounds. Then, with torn-up shirts, they made a big, clumsy bandage.

What chance was there for Silver, who lay with closed eyes, his face like a stone? How much life was flickering in him like a dying fire? Now and then his mouth pinched in a little, but there was no other way in which he expressed the agony that must be wringing him.

Beside him crouched the great wolf, making strange sounds in the base of his throat. The smell of blood,

146

even of his master's blood, made the slaver of the brute start running, and increased the fire in his eyes. But the sound in his throat was like a queer mourning. Sometimes he showed his great fangs, as though he would sink his teeth in the hands that worked over his master and gave him pain, but he seemed to realize that this work might be, beyond his comprehension, in behalf of Jim Silver.

Wayland could see, in the back of his mind, a picture of the dead man stretched here, unknown to the world, with the wolf keeping guard over the corpse, and the stallion lingering, starving among the rocks, unwilling to drift away from the body of Jim Silver.

Somewhere, in an old poem, there was such a picture. Somewhere in an old ballad. As though to prove that beasts may be truer than men.

When the bandaging was done, Lovell said eagerly:

"You can see for yourself. There ain't more'n a spark of life in him. He's going out. And every minute those three are getting closer. Listen!"

He sprang up and lifted his head to catch the sounds that drifted through the air. It was the clangor of iron-shod hoofs, far away, striking against a rocky surface. The noise poured closer and closer, seemed to sweep up the narrows of the ravine toward them, and then suddenly diminished and rolled away.

"They've gone by," sighed Lovell, with a groan of relief. "But they'll come again. Bray's got a brain in his head. Mantry is a devil. Lister has all the brains in the world. They'll find out they've drawn a blank, and they'll come back and find us! Wayland, this gent, Silver, has hounded fifty men to death. He's getting his own turn now, and I'm glad of it! That's what I say for myself. Let's clear out of here. We can climb that slope. In twenty minutes

147

we'll be where the three of 'em will never find us!"

His hand, that had stretched out toward the saddlebag, jumped back again as he saw the leveled gun of Wayland.

"I'll tell you something, brother," said Wayland. "Now that Silver's here, he's going to stay here. Fill your canteen out of that run of water, will you? And bring it over here. I won't leave him while he's alive. And when he's dead, I'll stay to burn him. He's got no claim on you, but he's got a claim on me. Understand? I won't leave him—not for half a billion dollars!"

Lovell, as he listened, swayed a little, as though the words were ponderous weights that he could hardly sustain. He swayed to this side and to that, making short, feeble gestures of protest. Then he remained silent, staring.

Wayland, looking beyond him, saw the moonlight brighten down the opposite slope of the little valley. They were caught in a funnel, as it were, and the moonlight would shine with increasing force, leaving only this slice of blackness where Jim Silver was stretched under the lip of the lower rock.

"All right," said Lovell finally, and his voice was no more than a whisper. "But listen!"

Once more they heard the ringing sound of hoofbeats out of the distance, slowly, slowly drawing back toward them.

"They'll block the ravine and then—"

Lovell said no more. He rose, gradually straightening his lithe body. He went to the run of water, filled his canteen, and brought it back.

Wayland took it. Lovell turned away and stood staring down the ravine, while Wayland, with one hand, lifted the fallen head of Jim Silver, and with the other

148

offered the canteen to his lips.

Silver drank eagerly.

Then he lay back, breathing hard, his eyes half open.

"How is it?" murmured Wayland.

"It's as if—the water—were blood—new blood. It's as if—I had a chance," breathed Silver.

He made a small gesture with his hand. Wayland took it in a strong grip. Tears rushed into Wayland's eyes.

"Old son!" he said through his teeth.

He saw Silver smile, and watched the eyes of the wounded man close again. The breast of Silver rose. He sighed. Peace seemed to be coming over him.

To Wayland, matters of life and death were suddenly given a new proportion. Death itself was no longer a frightful skeleton, a bogy. And life was no crown of glory. Death could be better than life. Dying in a good cause seemed itself the highest reward that could come to any man.

That had been the conviction of Jim Silver, Wayland knew. Because he thought nothing of himself, other men had loved him. Dumb beasts loved him, too.

Parade came and thrust out his long neck, and bent until his knees trembled with his weight and with horror at the smell of his master's blood. He snuffed at the face of Jim Silver, and then raised his head suddenly, and seemed about to whinny.

But there was only the tremor of the nostrils and no more. He had not been trained in vain by Jim Silver.

The wolf had risen when the horse drew near. Silently he had showed his fangs.

Now he lay down again, and dropped his head across the body of Silver. There he remained on watch while Wayland stood up to stretch his limbs.

There was a vague trouble in his mind. Finally he

realized that during all these last moments he had been completely unaware of Lovell—so unaware that the thief might have easily stolen the saddlebag again.

But the bag was still there. It was Lovell who was gone!

Softly Wayland ventured to call for him, and then more loudly. But Lovell was gone, and Wayland suddenly realized what his absence meant!

LOVELL'S TERMS

LOVELL WAS A LOGICIAN, AND HE KNEW MEN. THAT was why he left the wounded man and Wayland. The truth having once been shown to Lovell, he did not need to have a professor stand at a blackboard and point out the details of it. After he had brought the canteen of water to Wayland at his request, Lovell had stood for a moment with his back turned to the others and had considered matters afresh.

Then he stepped down the narrows of the ravine and went softly out of view. The matter was as clear as glass to him. He knew that Wayland was not talking for the sake of making an effect. He knew that Wayland would do exactly as he had said that he would do, and stay with the wounded man to the finish.

What would the finish be?

Well, Lovell could see that, too. He could see how the wounded man would grow weaker, the loss of blood wearing him down, while death was always assured for the end by the brutal fashion in which the bullet must have torn the interior of the body. Therefore big Jim Silver must die. But the gigantic strength of his body would draw out the struggle. He might even last two or three days. There had been known men who lingered through such a period of agony.

During all of that time Bray and the other two would be searching, searching all the while, and at last they would have daylight to aid them. By daylight they would re-follow the sign of the fugitives. They would spot the long strides by which the stallion had flown up the outer valley. They would distinguish his trail from the others, and thereby know that they were following the right direction. So, at last, they would turn the proper way—and behold, the dying man would be waiting for them, and the poor, clumsy, sentimental fool, Wayland, and also, there would be a wolf to be shot, a glorious stallion to be taken; and, last of all, and sweetest of all, half a million dollars for discreet hands to take and to spend.

Lover saw all of these things clearly. And suddenly he was ashamed. He was ashamed that he should be found on a side that must lose, and he was delighted that he saw a way of transferring himself to the winners. Of course, he could sneak away across the hills and thereby save his own hide. He could disappoint the dear vengeance of Bray and the others, to begin with. But was that enough?

No, there remained the money stolen from the Elkdale bank, which had once been all his, and to which he would still be able to put in a quarter claim.

Being a logical fellow and having a swift mind, he knew very exactly what he would do at the time he turned away from the wounded man, Wayland, the horse, and the wolf. He walked straight down the ravine and came to the outer valley.

Being broader, and running more to east and west, it took a fuller flood of the moonlight. So he picked out a

151

rock in the center of the valley and sat down there and made a cigarette.

What he thought about at that time was the face of Joe Mantry most of all.

Of course, all of the others hated him most heartily, but neither of the other two had the possibilities of hate developed to such a degree as Joe. Joe Mantry, when he saw the traitor, would go almost mad with the desire to kill. The other two would have to restrain him, because they would know that Lovell was not appearing before their eyes for fun. That would be the making of the comedy which Lovell would enjoy.

Afterward he would exact the faith of the three according to fearful oaths. And when he had done that, he would lead them to their prey. Now that he thought over all the elements of this comedy, it seemed to Lovell the most delightful thing that he had ever conceived.

He did exactly as he had planned. Sitting on the stone, he lighted his cigarette, and remained there even when he heard the rattling of hoofs coming toward him.

Then a single rider came into view—a big man with square-set shoulders. That would be Bray, and Bray was the man he most wanted to see.

It *was Bray*. He charged straight at the solitary figure which sat so moveless upon the stone, and when he was close to Lovell he uttered a shout of surprise.

Two more riders were in view by this time, but that didn't matter. Bray was not essentially a man of blood. He would not act until he knew why Lovell had dared to show himself. And he would keep the other two in hand. Rash and head-long as Joe Mantry was, Lovell knew that he dreaded death far less than he dreaded the strong nature of Bray.

152

So Lovell remained seated, carefully smoking his cigarette and blowing the smoke over his head into the moonlight, while Bray dismounted before him and covered him with a gun.

"Well, Lovell," said Bray, "I've been wanting to meet you for a long time."

"I decided that I'd give you boys a break," was Lovell's answer.

He was proud of that answer. He was so proud that he began to smile, and he was still smiling when Dave Lister and Mantry came up. That smile of his was what held their hands. They could not believe what they saw.

"All right," said Bray. "We're not here for our health. What have you got to say?"

"What do you want to hear?" asked Lovell, looking squarely at Bray.

"I want to hear where I can pick up half a million in ready cash," said Bray quietly.

"I could tell you that," said Lovell.

"We're listening," said Bray.

"We make some terms first," said Lovell.

"Terms?" shouted Joe Mantry. "Terms with you, you rat?"

"You take an oath, all of you. That's what I mean," said Lovell. "Beginning with Joe Mantry, you take an oath."

"I'll see you—" began Mantry.

"You'll take an oath," repeated Lovell.

"I don't care what happens," said Mantry. "I've got you here. And I know what to do with you. You others turn your backs for a minute."

"Listen," said Bray. "Don't be a fool, Joe. You don't think he's out here unless he has something to sell, do you?"

The thing was too obvious. Mantry groaned and turned his back.

"I'll show you the half million," said Lovell. "But first we all shake hands. We shake hands that the past is forgotten, that nobody ever damns me for anything I've ever done, that nobody ever throws it up to me, that the three of you stand by me like a pal, and that I get a one-fourth cut in the loot."

Mantry cried out in exquisite pain at the thought.

"Beginning with Joe, we shake hands," said Lovell, grinning.

He had decided, on deliberation, that nothing would be as good as a handshake. If those fellows could drive themselves to shaking hands with him, the future would be safe for Lovell.

Mantry whirled about and said:

"I'll see you—"

"Steady!" said Bray. "You see how things are, Joe. What's the use of cutting your own throat for the sake of Jimmy, here? What's the use of throwing a hundred thousand plus out the window? Can't you use a bit of chicken feed like that?"

Those words had their own weight. Mantry groaned again, but suddenly he gave a tug to the brim of his hat, stepped up, and held out his hand.

"I hate your dirty heart, and you know it," he said. "Nothing will ever stop me from hating it. But here's my hand, and I'll stand by what I do with it."

Lovell took that hand with a nameless relief in his heart. Lister gave his next, silently. Bray said, as he shook hands:

"I never expected to do this. But you're a bright fellow, Jimmy."

"Sure I am," said Jimmy Lovell confidently.

Then he made another cigarette and lighted it.

"They're in there," he said. "Wayland's in there, and the half million in the saddlebag. And Jim Silver!"

There was a quick, subdued chorus of exclamations. "Silver!"

The three looked at one another, and Lovell enjoyed their dismay for a moment. The half million that had seemed to be in their hands was now jerked off to a distance, as it were.

Then Mantry said: "We gave our hands on condition that the half million should be handed over. There was no talk of any Jim Silver then."

Lovell laughed.

"The horse and the wolf and the man—they're all in there," he said. "But maybe you boys will be glad to know that after Silver stole Wayland away from you— what a lot of dumb birds you are to let him snake a man right out of the lot of you!—after he'd done that, a slug of lead happened to rap him. It tore right through him. He's lying now on his back, pretty nearly dead. He can just about open his eyes, and that's all. I thought that maybe you'd be glad to know about that!"

He looked at them and relished the sighs of relief.

"We can go right in, boys," said Jimmy Lovell. "I'll lead the way. They'll be down there at the head of the valley. They're laid up under a big rock—a cut-back at the bottom of a cliff. You can find 'em by yourselves, but I'll show you the way. Bray, lend me a gun."

He got a gun. Not a revolver. He wanted no nonsense like that in this sort of light for shooting. What he wanted was a rifle, and he got it.

"Now," said Jimmy Lovell, "I want you saps to understand that that fool of a Wayland is in there with Jim Silver. Fool is the right word. And he's ready to die

155

for his partner, Silver. I tell you, fellows, you'd better shoot straight at him. He's the one that matters, Silver don't count. We can blot him out of the picture any time, as soon as Wayland is out of the way. And when we've blotted out Jim Silver, will we have something to talk about the rest of our lives? Yes, we will. And a plenty lot, too!"

He laughed again as he said that. To blot out Jim Silver! Why, it would make heroes of them all. It hardly mattered that Jim Silver had been wounded and made helpless. It really mattered not at all. Nobody would ever know about that. All that other people would know would be that the great Jim Silver had been blotted out finally by Lovell and his three companions. In such a killing there was more than enough glory to serve them all around. Every crook in the West would heave a long, long breath of relief. No matter how the actual fight went, there would surely be enough talk afloat to make it into an epic battle. People would point out Jimmy Lovell hereafter. They would whisper to one another: "There goes the man who killed Jim Silver!"

An ecstasy came over Lovell. He was half blinded with joy. Tears came into his eyes. For the moment he had in him the stuff that heroes are made of, and he led the way right down through the darkness of the narrow ravine.

THE ATTACK

THERE WAS NOT MUCH OF THE BLOODY INSTINCT FOR battle in Wayland, but he had plenty of brains, notwithstanding. He was the sort of a fellow who could read in books and papers about the heroism of other

156

men and shudder to think of their greatness and his own lack of the divine fire. But he had a good head on his shoulders, and as he sat by Silver, pondering the disappearance of Jimmy Lovell and what it was likely to mean, he saw that there was only one answer to the problem.

There were several ways in which the ravine might be attacked if—as he suspected—Lovell had gone out to make his peace with the others and to lead them into the place where Jim Silver lay helpless and wounded. The best and the safest way would be to send at least one man up to the top of the height and let him command the whole battle arena with a rifle after he had posted himself among the rocks above.

Then the remainder could work their way down through the ravine and come to action with Wayland and his pitiful single rifle.

That was the logical way of going about things, but men who have great odds of numbers in their favor are not so apt to do things in the most intelligent way. Like strong bulls, they are apt to close their eyes and to rush straight forward. That was what the four crooks would do, Wayland was convinced. For they all knew that he was not a great fighter, and that he was probably a clumsy hand with weapons.

That was what convinced him that the best thing he could do was to leave his place of last retreat and to attack the enemy on the march if he could. Fight fire with fire. That was the way.

When he had made up his mind, he pulled the rifle out of the saddle scabbard on the big stallion. It was loaded, and in perfect condition, as every weapon in the possession of Silver was sure to be.

Now he stood up and looked wistfully down at the

face of the wounded man. The moonlight sloped into the cut-back. It did not reach Silver with its direct light, but it threw glittering reflections from the face of the quartzite rocks all around. Those reflections showed Silver like an image of cut stone. It showed him faintly smiling, the master of his pain even when he lay half senseless with the recently inflicted wound.

Now the eyes of the wounded man opened.

"Are you going, Wayland?" he asked in his quiet way.

The thought that he might be suspected of leaving his post tore the heart of Wayland. He dropped down on one knee and took the head of Silver.

"Not for long," he said. "I'm coming back—as soon as I can."

"All right," said Silver. "Good luck, old son."

Wayland turned away and walked rapidly from the end of the ravine until he came to the narrow throat of the little canyon, dodging the brush that half filled the place as he went along.

He picked out a spot where there was a small boulder—a small rock, but one that would cover him well enough. He lay down behind this and began to study the shadows before him.

The light was terribly treacherous. It seemed almost safer to try to shoot by starlight than by the partial glances which the moon threw into this gorge. Here it glimmered, and there it was gone. Here it painted the face of a rock with its blackest shadow, and there it gave out a glimmering from the crystals of the stone.

As he waited, he felt that this straining of his eyes at one object after another was accomplishing no good except to strain the optic nerve and bewilder his brain entirely. Yet he kept on pointing his rifle at one dim

158

target after another, calculating his aim, and steadying his nerves always for the trial that he was sure would come.

Something whispered over his head. It was the shadowy flight of an owl, cleaving the air with wings of an enormous size. Apollyon approached sometimes in the form of a night bird, the old books said. What is it that men see before their death? Only a few have had sufficient breath to gasp out a few words of revelation before their eyes are finally closed and their throats sealed.

It seemed to him that he had seen death actually in the air above him.

He recovered from his thoughts, and, staring down the ravine, suddenly he was aware of a man stepping out from a blackness of tall shrubbery. A man, and another, and another, and another. Not in single file, but in a soft-stepping group.

His heart raced. His eyes went black for an instant.

Then he leveled the rifle carefully. He took the leading form. His hands were shaking terribly. Then he fired.

The leader did not fall, but leaped instead. high into the air, and landed running. The other three were already scattering to either side. As he pumped lead at them rapidly, poor Wayland knew that he was missing with every shot.

But now they were out of sight. He heard voices cursing. It was his name that was being cursed. Then a silence followed. He strained eyes and ears from this side of the rock and then from the other. Every moment he expected to see four forms grow up out of the ground and charge at him to beat him down with a single powerful rush.

He had failed; he had failed! Would any other one of the lot of them have failed, given similar chances? He knew that they would not. They would not have had the dreadful shuddering of nerves and muscles as they leveled their weapons at human lives. Rather, they would have rejoiced!

Every moment now the gorge was beginning to be a place of greater danger, for as the moon mounted higher, it threw an increasing multitude of small and glinting lights into the interior.

Then something struck the sand beside him and threw the stuff in a shower over him, into his face, half blinding him. The report of the gun barked sharply in his ears.

It came from high up on the left-hand side of the ravine. He heard the triumphant yell of the marksman. Another bullet flattened on the rock before him. Another whirred through the air over his head, and a chorus of shouts broke out from the three men who remained in hiding down the valley.

Well, they had him, all right, and he knew it. He stared at the winking fire flashes of the gun up the side of the ravine, and did not even try to answer the bullets. There was no use. The fellow was sure to have perfect cover. Wayland's rock was no longer a protection to him, but if he dared to get up and bolt to the rear, that would be the very thing that the three men down the valley were waiting for. And they would riddle him with bullets as he ran.

Had they already come in behind him? Something certainly moved among the brush behind him and to the left.

He stared with dread in that direction, and then he made out the nodding head of a horse. Next he saw a strange sight indeed through a gap in the brush where the moonlight fell sheer down.

He saw Parade walking slowly forward. He saw a body dragging from one stirrup. And then he made out that it was Jim Silver who was being so oddly transported. There had not been strength enough in him to walk, but, like a good soldier, when he heard the noise of guns, he had to go toward it. Therefore he had perhaps ordered the stallion to kneel beside him, and, getting a grip with his teeth on the bottom of the stirrup leather, he had managed to order the horse to rise again and to go forward.

For that was what was happening, and Parade was marching into the battle, dragging his master at his feet. Wayland could see the gleaming of the naked revolver which dragged, also, in the hand of Silver. And at the side of the man skulked the great wolf, looking a great deal like a form of the moonlight when it struck on his pale-gray fur.

Yes, that was the miracle that appeared for a few seconds through the gap in the brush and was lost to view again.

Then another bullet from the marksman up the slope snatched the hat from the head of Wayland. The very next shot of all would scatter his brains, no doubt. He worked a bit to one side. Down the valley the men were laughing. He could hear their voices. He could distinguish the high, whining mirth of Lovell.

Once more the marksman up the side of the ravine fired, and something like a hot knife slashed through the surface flesh of Wayland's side.

He gathered himself. It was better to charge straight into the face of danger than to lie still and be shot to pieces. He would charge—and Jim Silver would see him die!

Then, out of the brush to his left, a gun spoke.

It was not aimed at Wayland. There was no sound of whirring lead. But high up the side of the ravine there was an answering scream of agony.

A figure leaped up from among the rocks and tottered into the full light of the moon—Joe Mantry, walking with his arms flung out and his head back, like one who feels his way in the dark. A warning chorus yelled at Mantry from down the ravine. But he walked straight on, stepped out into space, and then pitched forward.

A frightful moment elapsed. The shadow covered the falling body. But Wayland distinctly heard the loose shock and jar as it met the ground.

Joe Mantry was dead.

And Wayland knew that Jim Silver had managed to strike one blow at the enemy. Ah, if only a tenth part of his real strength were in him, how he would scatter the three men who were left down the valley!

"He's shifted over to the left!" some one called.

Was that not Lovell? Yet, it must be Lovell, yelling:

"Charge in here on the right, boys. Come on in. We'll cut him off. We'll tear him to pieces!"

"Look out! There's two of 'em!" called the heavy voice of Bray.

"Aw, Silver's as good as dead!" cried Lovell. "Come on, you cowards, and I'll show you the way to do it."

He came right out through the shadows, bending over, running low, with his rifle swinging back and forth as he raced. Right at Wayland's rock he charged, while two other forms leaped out from the brush and pursued him in the effort.

Wayland took a good aim—and the hammer of the gun dropped with a dull click! Something had gone

162

wrong with the mechanism. He might have known better than to leave it open to the flying sprays of sand, perhaps!

But again the revolver of Jim Silver spoke from the side.

Lovell stopped running, spun around, and, while he was still spinning, a second shot found him in the shadows and dropped him in a moveless heap to the ground.

Again that terrible gunman to the left of Wayland fired, and this time the tall body of Dave Lister leaped up and jackknifed in the air. He fell to the ground and lay there perfectly still.

Silver's gun was still flaming, and its last bullet found the heart of big Phil Bray. He slumped down, his lifeless body sprawling over a small boulder.

THE RETURN

THERE WAS NO QUESTION OF MOVING JIM SILVER from the spot where Wayland found him afterward, stretched on his face in a dead faint. His exertions had caused his wounds to burst out into a fresh tide of bleeding. He was quite unconscious.

A day later he was able to speak again.

Two days after that he was lost in the madness of a high fever. And it was still another week before he opened his eyes and looked out with a clear vision upon the world.

Wayland had buried the four dead men in the meantime. He had taken their effects and wrapped them in a slicker, so that the law would be able to identify the four wrongdoers. He had to take other time out from his care of Silver in order to hunt and then to cook. And day and night there was hardly a moment when he dared to close his eyes.

Finally he dared to move Jim Silver. The wounds were not healing as they ought to, and Wayland guessed, when the fever continued even after the delirium ended, that the wounds were deeply infected, and that expert medical attendance was necessary.

So he made a horse litter out of the lean, limber poles of saplings and stretched a blanket across it. On that comfortable contrivance he stretched Silver. His own horse took the lead. And sure-footed Parade followed, with the butt ends of the saplings tied into his stirrup leathers.

That was the fashion in which Wayland made his march up the ravines and out into sight of the town of Elkdale.

People never forgot the procession as it turned down the main street of the town, with a tall, gaunt form leading a runt of a mustang, a man with a shaggy, new growth of unrazored beard on his face, and his hollow eyes burning with triumph and joy. At the tail of the mustang swung the light litter, and in that litter lay a man at whose side skulked what seemed a huge gray timber wolf. Except that who has ever heard of a tame lobo?

But, last of all, bringing up the procession, and identifying the man who lay in the litter, pranced a great chestnut stallion on whose silken sides the sun flamed eagerly.

That was Parade. Every man and boy, every woman and child, had seen pictures of the glorious horse, and they knew him now.

They came out and walked at a respectful distance

from the procession, for the whisper went through the air and reached every heart: Silver himself lay in the litter, wounded very badly, dying, perhaps.

They walked with hushed murmurs until the mustang was guided to the door of the doctor's house.

There many willing, gentle, respectful hands loosed the litter. They had a dangerous time doing their work, for Frosty, though terrified by the presence of such great numbers of the enemy, man, was ready to tear them all to pieces. It required the steady, gentle voice of his master to keep him in hand. Even so, the bearers of that litter walked on tiptoe as they carried their famous burden into the doctor's house.

They laid him on the doctor's own big, comfortable double bed at the doctor's request. Frosty installed himself instantly on the rug at the bedside; and the stallion, Parade, was loosed in the little plot of pasture ground where the doctor's cow grazed.

So, Parade, from time to time, could thrust his head right in over the sill of the window and whinny very softly, now and again, to his master. On those occasions the great wolf was sure to rise up and bare his teeth with a terrible snarl. He never shared his master willingly with the horse. He never shared Silver willingly with any human company, either, and from first to last he had his teeth bared when even tall Wayland came stepping into the room.

As for Silver, the wide-whiskered doctor pronounced a favorable verdict at once. He declared that Silver should have died, of course, during the first fever, but since that was ended, it was merely a matter of antiseptics and a little patience and care.

Patience and care? The whole town of Elkdale was ready to offer its services. It was ready to watch by day and by night.

Then came the day when Rucker and his daughter arrived.

It was a great day for Wayland. It was such a great day that he wanted to sneak away from the meeting, because he did not know how he should be able to endure the thanks of the banker for what he had done.

But Rucker took that famous saddlebag with the treasure inside it and threw it profanely into a corner.

"It don't make a bit of difference to me," he said. "I'm through with the banking business. I can raise all the beef I can eat on my ranch. I can get all the happiness I want out of my own mountains. And what will I be doing with half a million in spare cash? I don't owe it to anybody. My depositors didn't lose a bean. This here is nothing but a lot of extra capital for you, Wayland."

"Capital for me?" said Wayland, aghast.

"What do you mean by that tone?" asked the banker. "Don't you intend to marry May, or have you only been philandering with her? May, come here. Here's a hound that's only been wasting your time. He didn't mean a word that he spoke."

Well, it was possible for Wayland to explain that he had meant every word of it. He took the girl in to see Jim Silver, and Silver smiled at her quietly and took her hand:

"You've got the best sort of a man in the world," he told her. "Because he's always better than the best he knows about himself."

We hope that you enjoyed reading this
Sagebrush Large Print Western.
If you would like to read more Sagebrush titles,
ask your librarian or contact the Publishers:

United States and Canada

Thomas T. Beeler, *Publisher*
Post Office Box 659
Hampton Falls, New Hampshire 03844-0659
(800) 818-7574

United Kingdom, Eire, and
the Republic of South Africa

Isis Publishing Ltd
7 Centremead
Osney Mead
Oxford OX2 0ES England
(01865) 250333

Australia and New Zealand

Bolinda Publishing Pty. Ltd.
17 Mohr Street
Tullamarine, 3043, Victoria, Australia
(016103) 9338 0666